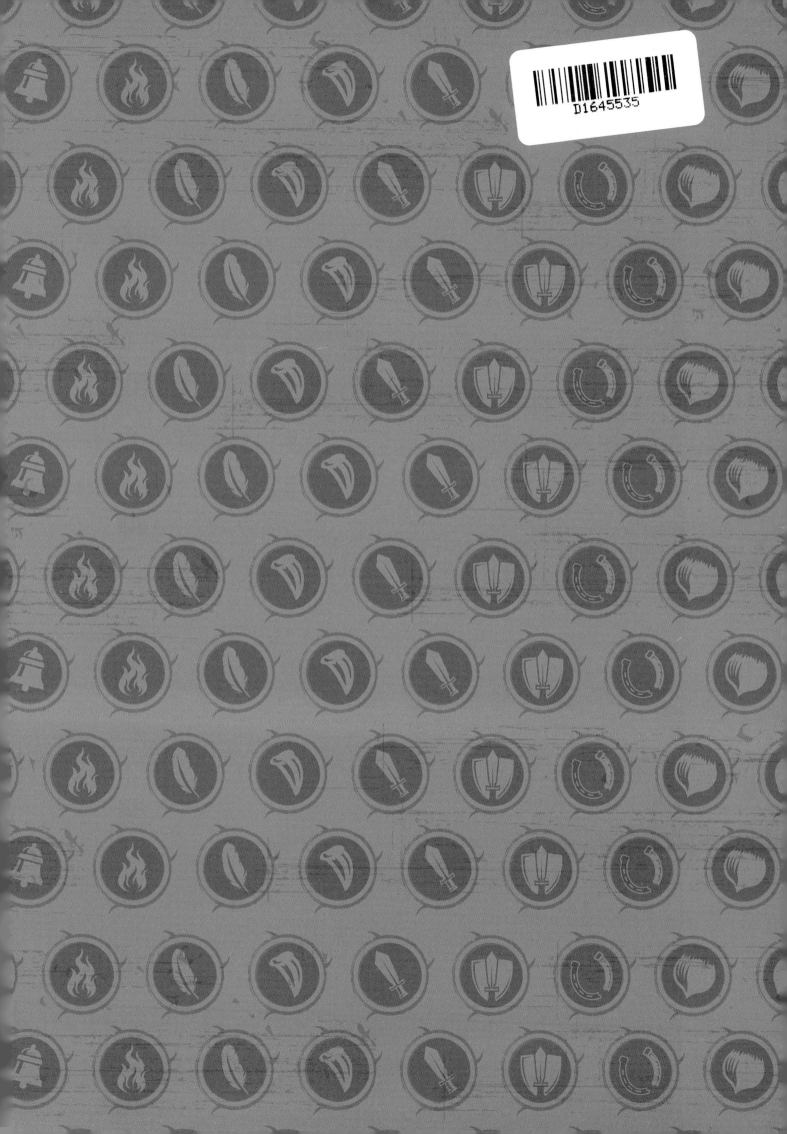

CONTENTS

Ⓟ PROFILE

Ⓢ STORY

Ⓜ KINGDOM MAP

Pedigree®

PUBLISHED 2014. PEDIGREE BOOKS LIMITED, BEECH HILL HOUSE, WALNUT GARDENS, EXETER, DEVON EX4 4DH.

WWW.PEDIGREEBOOKS.COM – BOOKS@PEDIGREEGROUP.CO.UK

THE PEDIGREE TRADEMARK, EMAIL AND WEBSITE ADDRESSES, ARE THE SOLE AND EXCLUSIVE PROPERTIES OF PEDIGREE GROUP LIMITED, USED UNDER LICENCE IN THIS PUBLICATION.

Welcome, brave followers of the Quest, to the kingdom of Avantia! In this Annual, you will learn all about the adventures that Elenna and I have undertaken in the past, in our never-ending efforts to keep Avantia and other realms free from the clutches of Evil. While I hope you find them exciting, you must remember that Beast Quests are very dangerous, and are never to be taken lightly.

You will also have your wits tested with some fiendish games and puzzles, and receive step-by-step instructions on how to make special items that you might, one day, need on a Quest of your own. Destiny and Danger may be in your future, so…

Stay brave, always,

Tom

THE STORY SO FAR...

BEAST QUEST...

My adventures began when my home village, Errinel was struck by a series of mysterious fires. Everyone was very worried — we were a farming community, and crops were badly damaged. My uncle, Henry, said that someone needed to travel to Avantia's capital and ask for the king's help. I had no hesitation in volunteering — this sounded like just the sort of adventure I had been waiting for my whole life... the kind of adventure that would make my father proud.

In time, I would find out why I had never known my father, Taladon, when I was growing up; but back then, all I knew was that he had gone off on a mission one day, and had never returned.

When I reached The City — after a very long walk — I was dismayed to see that people from all over the kingdom had showed up, begging for assistance. Errinel was counting on me, so I decided to take matters into my own hands. I sneaked into the king's palace and posed as a servant, hoping that if I could speak to His Majesty directly, then he would send help to Errinel.

As I sneaked around the palace, I overheard the king talking about the death of a knight, who had fallen during a battle with a... dragon! It was the Beast that had been burning crops in the kingdom, but the king ordered that this be kept secret from the people — no one could know that the Beasts were real.

Brave I may have been, but I was definitely not stealthy — the king's guards caught me eavesdropping. I probably would have been locked up or kicked out of the city, had Avantia's wise old Wizard, Aduro, not assured the king that I could be trusted to save the kingdom. Somehow, he recognized me as the son of Taladon, Avantia's bravest warrior.

Arming me with a sword, a shield — and a courageous stallion called Storm — Aduro sent me on my way. It was my first Beast Quest — but it would definitely not be my last.

My route to the dragon's lair took me by the Forest of Fear, where I helped a girl and her pet wolf evade capture by soldiers. She joined me on my Quest to free Ferno the Fire Dragon, who had been placed under an evil spell by the Dark Wizard, Malvel — Aduro's enemy. After we broke the spell on Ferno, we set about freeing the other five Beasts, travelling to every corner of the kingdom... or so we thought!

THE GOLDEN ARMOUR...

I do sometimes wonder what my Uncle Leo thought about me disappearing. One day, I left our fishing village in the southwest of the kingdom to go hunting in the Forest of Fear — and I didn't return for a very long time.

The Golden Armour is a precious Avantian artefact, and I was determined to recover it for the kingdom. I was honoured and proud to wear it — but I only had it for a short time. As I would soon discover, the Armour belonged to someone else...

I know Aduro made sure to send word to Leo, so that he knew where I was, but I still feel bad about making him worry.

Anyway — after we freed the six Good Beasts from his magic, Malvel launched another attack on the kingdom. This time, he stole the six pieces of the Golden Armour. This suit protects Avantia's Master of the Beasts, who is the only person who can wear it, and use the magical powers it provides. Malvel scattered the pieces all over Avantia. They were to be guarded by six Beasts — but these Beasts were not Evil because they had been placed under a spell. These Beasts were Evil by nature!

It was an even tougher task than our first Quest, but we had tricks of our own to use against Malvel — now that he had freed the Good Beasts, Tom could call upon them whenever he was in serious trouble! All he had to do was touch one of the tokens in his shield, and that Beast would appear to help Tom battle Malvel's Evil Beast.

When Tom defeated the final Beast — Trillion — the Three-headed Lion's body transformed into a Gateway to another realm... This realm was the terrifying kingdom of Gorgonia — a lawless, anarchic world guarded by Evil Beasts, and ripped apart by a civil war that raged beneath its terrible red sky. But we could not turn away from this battle — Malvel had used his cruel magic to lure Avantia's Good Beasts to Gorgonia, where they were kept prisoner by Malvel's most evil and vicious Beasts yet. For each Beast he vanquished, Tom would be gifted a precious jewel to place into his Jewelled Belt. Each one gave him new magical powers — like the ability to communicate with Beasts, or to heal broken bones. Now, Tom felt as though no Quest would ever be too difficult.

But he was wrong...

THE AMULET OF AVANTIA...

After returning from Gorgonia, Tom and Elenna joined King Hugo's army. Elenna taught archery to the recruits, while Tom was a fine soldier — even though Captain Harkman, the grumpy cadet officer, called him a slacker.

Tom's life changed forever the moment a call went up across the palace — "Taladon has returned!" Tom was excited to finally meet his father after all this time, but there was a sting in this tale — Taladon was half-ghost! I explained to Tom that he could rescue his father by reclaiming all six pieces of the Amulet of Avantia, which Malvel had long ago broken — but to do that, he would need to defeat the six Ghost Beasts that guarded them. Tom proved equal to the challenge, and he banished Malvel from Avantia. We hoped it would be for good. But it was not...

Now that Taladon had returned, he reclaimed his position as Master of the Beasts. But that did not mean my Beast Quests were over. There were other kingdoms in trouble, besides Avantia, and my adventures took me across the Western Ocean, to a kingdom called Gwildor. Here, I found a new Dark Wizard enemy — Velmal — who had used his magic to corrupt the Good Beasts.

It was not just Velmal I faced down, but also Gwildor's Mistress of the Beasts. Freya was also under the Dark Wizard's spell, which had transformed her into a wicked, cunning minion of Evil. I would soon discover the shocking truth — Freya was my long-lost mother! But before I could rescue her, Velmal ripped open a portal and dragged her through. Elenna and I followed, without a clue where we were going!

We found ourselves in the kingdom of Kayonia — a realm that had been plunged into chaos and darkness. Now, we had to find the ingredients that would make up the antidote that would save my mother's life, as well as free Kayonia from the wrath of terrifying Beasts. We pursued Velmal all over Kayonia, until we finally arrived at the capital city, Meaton, which was under attack from a plague of wasps commanded by the final Beast — Vespick the Wasp Queen. After defeating Vespick, we freed my mother from Velmal's magic once and for all. Our Quest complete, I wanted to take my mother to Avantia, to reunite her with my father. We stepped through a new portal that would take us home...

THE LOST WORLD...

We thought were returning to Avantia, but we were wrong. The place where we had ended up was not Tom's home kingdom — it was actually a strange mirror of Avantia, called Tavania. It looked almost identical — except it was a place where Taladon never became a hero, so the Beasts here were vulnerable to Dark Magic, which had dragged them out of their natural habitats. This was very bad news, because Tavania was where Malvel had disappeared to after Tom last defeated him. When we arrived, Malvel had us thrown in his palace dungeons — after he had used his magic to kill Aduro's young Wizard apprentice, Marc! After escaping from the dungeon, we went our separate ways — Tom and Elenna travelled the kingdom, returning the Beasts to their rightful homes, while I trained up the lazy mirror-version of Taladon to be the hero his kingdom deserved. Once we had completed this Quest, we re-opened a portal and Tom took Malvel back to Avantia — he was to be thrown into the dungeons! But the portal closed too quickly...

The portal closed too quickly, leaving behind Tom's mother... and my wolf, Silver! Not even seeing Malvel finally arrested for all his crimes could make us feel better now. Even though Taladon went searching for the magical Tree of Being — which Aduro said was going to be the key to getting Silver and Freya back — days passed with no sign of them. And our hearts sank even lower when Taladon returned to the palace, bloodied from a battle with the Pirates of Makai — a ruthless band of cutthroats, who were also looking for the Tree. Their leader was Sanpao, who captained a flying pirate ship and commanded six of the most frightening Beasts we had encountered. It all came down to a final battle in the Palace courtyard, where the Tree of Being had magically sprouted. We protected it from the Pirate King, and were rewarded by the return of our lost friends...But our troubles were not over.

Malvel was devious, and used the distraction of the courtyard battle to make his escape from the dungeon. With his new apprentice, a young Witch called Petra, he fled to the distant, mysterious kingdom of Seraph — and he had taken the Warlock's Staff. A magical artefact, made of wood from the Tree of Being, the Staff was a powerful magical tool in the right hands — and potentially deadly in the wrong. Malvel's hands were definitely the wrong hands! But, once more, we were able to defeat him, stealing back the Staff and casting the Dark Wizard into a magical fire known as the Eternal Flame...But it would still not be the last we saw of him...

THE STORY SO FAR... CONTINUED

MASTER OF THE BEASTS...

We thought we had defeated Malvel once and for all, but we were wrong. The Dark Wizard was unable to set foot back in Avantia, but that did not mean he couldn't wreak more havoc in the kingdom... and this time, he had put in motion his most diabolical plan. Two days after Elenna and I returned from Seraph, an earthquake struck The City. With Aduro, we ventured down to the Gallery of Tombs — a vast mausoleum where great Avantian heroes are buried. We discovered that six marble tombs had been broken open, and were now empty! Aduro explained these were the tombs of the Knights of Forton — fabled warriors who had fought alongside Tanner, first Master of the Beasts. Legend said they would arise again when Avantia faced its darkest hour. But this time, they would not be protecting us — they would be bringing the darkness to the kingdom. Malvel's magic had unleashed the six terrible Beasts the Knights were famous for defeating — and now, the warriors and their enemies had merged into one, able to change shape from man to Beast. And what was worse, they had split up, taking separate courses as they brought destruction to the kingdom — and with my parents away from Avantia on special missions for Aduro, Elenna and I were on our own. All over Avantia we travelled, fighting Beasts at every turn, and using the Knights' own weapons to defeat them. The penultimate leg of this Quest took us to the Icy Plains of Avantia's northland, and it would be there where our Beast Quests truly saw their Darkest Hour...

What happened next is still too painful for Tom to talk about. By now, Taladon had returned to Avantia, and joined us on our Quest. We were to face Tecton, who had merged with the White Knight. The White Knight set fire to Nanook's snow cave, trapping her inside, and sought to keep Tom occupied by challenging him to a joust. But Taladon stepped up instead, so Tom could free Nanook. Sadly, it would be the final brave choice of Taladon's heroic life.

The White Knight, riding his varkule, was too mighty even for Tom's father, and Taladon died in battle. As his body was spirited away to the Gallery of Tombs, the magical Golden Armour appeared around Tom. He was now officially Master of the Beasts, but he was heartbroken that this honour had come at the cost of his father's life. His first act as Master was to avenge Taladon's death by defeating Tecton and the White Knight. Then he bested the Golden Knight and his Beast, Doomskull, who had laid siege to The City, before Ferno — the first Beast Tom ever encountered — answered my call, and drove Malvel out of Avantia. This time, it was for good.

THE STORY SO FAR...
CONTINUED

THE NEW AGE...

It was a rainy day when Taladon's coffin was taken to the Gallery of Tombs, to rest in peace beside his predecessors. But there was no time for us to mourn — in the kingdom of Henkrall, a new enemy was preparing to attack Avantia. Her name was Kensa, and she was an Evil Sorceress banished to Henkrall by the Circle of Wizards, who disapproved of her meddling with forbidden magic. Now, she had stolen blood from Avantia's Good Beasts to take back to Henkrall so that she could create six Beasts of her own — Beasts who would bend to her Evil will...

To get us to Henkrall, Aduro gave us a magical staff, and then told us to go outside... and wait to be struck by lightning! The Lightning Path took us to Henkrall. We were without our usual animal companions, but we found faithful replacements in a black wolf named Spark, and a purple horse named Tempest, who were perfect for getting around Henkrall, because they had wings! In fact, all the people and animals in Henkrall had wings — except for Kensa, and her one-eyed, hunchbacked minion, Igor. After we defeated her six Beasts, Kensa tried to travel to Avantia via The Lightning Path, but we made sure to follow her. We ended up back in Avantia's City, and the Sorceress was taken to the dungeons — but we were to find out that this had been her plan all along. With her longtime companion, Sanpao, Kensa made an escape!

LIGHTNING TOKENS

These curious artefacts might not look like much, but they saved our skins many times! The White Token can shatter eardrums, while the Golden Token can wound even the sturdiest of Beast-flesh. My favourite, though, was the Blue Token — when the giant shark, Solak, swallowed me whole, it was this object which saved me when its energy exploded Solak from within, turning the Beast into thousands of tiny bubbles!

BLUE LIGHTNING TOKEN

A glowing blue orb filled with explosive energy that Tom can use to get himself out of a tight spot.

Age	261
Power	184
Magic Level	176
Fright Factor	83

WHITE LIGHTNING TOKEN

A white glassy orb that can shatter the eardrum of even the fiercest Beast.

Age	30
Power	75
Magic Level	148
Fright Factor	53

PURPLE LIGHTNING TOKEN

This purple crystal can undo even the sturdiest of structures.

Age	30
Power	81
Magic Level	143
Fright Factor	54

ORANGE LIGHTNING TOKEN

This magical orange gemstone can power complex machinery - use it wisely, for it might be the only thing that can save your life.

Age	30
Power	76
Magic Level	165
Fright Factor	45

RED LIGHTNING TOKEN

Shield your eyes if this Lightning Token explodes - it will be the only way to save your eyesight!

Age	30
Power	74
Magic Level	150
Fright Factor	65

GOLDEN LIGHTNING TOKEN

Not even Beast flesh can withstand the awesome power of this Lightning Token.

Age	30
Power	80
Magic Level	170
Fright Factor	60

THE WARRIOR'S ROAD...

With the Pirate King and the Sorceress at large, we knew we had to set off after them immediately — but our plans were thwarted. First, Aduro was arrested by the Circle of Wizards, who stripped him of his magic as punishment for using the illegal Lightning Path! Second, our use of the Path had wounded reality, and dragged Avantia, Gorgonia and Kayonia closer together — when they were supposed to be in separate dimensions! It was our most dangerous Quest yet — if we failed, the three kingdoms would stay chaotically merged forever...

Our most recent Quests united Avantia's troubled past with its future — which I hope will be a triumphant one! We hoped that The Circle of Wizards were done meddling in Avantian affairs after they drained Aduro of his magic — but their leader, The Judge (who we would discover to be in league with Kensa and Sanpao) had more nasty tricks up his sleeve. In an effort to make sure Avantia had no protection from Beasts, The Judge reinstated a forgotten magical rule that demanded anyone who wanted to be Master or Mistress of the Beasts had to complete the most dangerous and deadly Quest of all — The Warrior's Road. On this Quest, we would walk in the footsteps of some of Avantia's bravest heroes — and many more who were not fortunate enough to survive. The Road was haunted by the spirit of Tanner, Avantia's very first Master of the Beasts, whose fate remained a secret only Avantia's greatest warriors could ever know...

After we drove The Judge out of Avantia — we hope for good! — we next ventured to Rion, where an old friend needed our help. Wilfred was the Beast Keeper, whose job it was to look after the youngest Beasts in the kingdoms as they learned how to control their immense powers. But Kensa had struck again, using a hideous poison called Lunar Blood to enslave the six youngest Beasts in Rion — including Vedra and Krimon, the Twin Dragons we had rescued as babies on one of our earliest Quests. Only Vedra, the Green Dragon, had not turned to Evil after Kensa had wrought her wicked vengeance on Rion, but if Elenna and I did not save him before the next Full Moon, Vedra would be Evil as well! We had to find the four ingredients of the Gilded Elixir — the only known antidote to Lunar Blood. But, to do this, we would have to battle our young Beast friends, who now saw us as enemies. One by one, we outwitted the Beasts of Rion, and in defeat, they were restored to Good. We were able to heal Vedra with the Gilded Elixir, and the Green Dragon arose to face off against his twin brother in a battle for the kingdom...

TOM

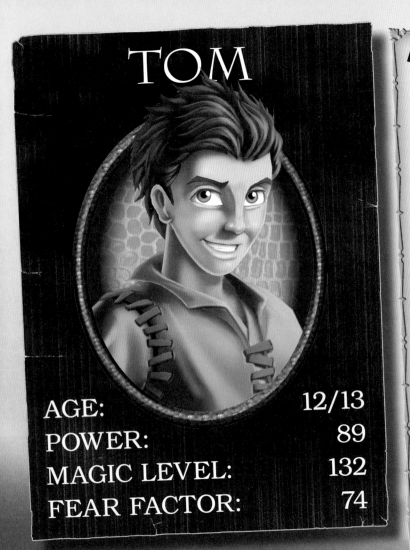

AGE: 12/13
POWER: 89
MAGIC LEVEL: 132
FEAR FACTOR: 74

Tom is the bravest young hero in Avantia, who has fought tirelessly to protect the Kingdom from Evil attacks. He was born in the village of Errinel, and was raised by his blacksmith uncle, Henry, and his aunt Maria. After venturing to The City to ask the king to provide help for his village, and being charged with saving Avantia from Beast-attacks, Tom has barely rested — in fact, the days when he does not have a Quest to complete are days when he gets frightfully bored! Indeed, he once got so bored that he joined the king's army — although he had to pretend to be more tired from exercises than he actually was, because his duties fighting Beasts was a secret back then!

After the death of his father, Tom inherited the role of Master of the Beasts, becoming the latest in a long line of courageous Avantian warriors that stretches all the way back to Tanner. Tom vows to give his all to protecting the kingdom, every day — a Master of the Beasts gets no days off, and he wants no days off!

BEST MOMENTS:

- Aduro recognising me as the son of Taladon!
- Meeting Elenna for the first time in the Forest of Fear.
- Rescuing two baby dragons and making sure they were kept safe from Evil.
- Reuniting with my father and mother.
- Saving Tanner, the First Master, from his torment, and allowing him to rest in peace.

WORST MOMENTS:

- Krabb's poisonous bite — I almost lost my hand!
- Finding out that Velmal had enslaved my mother.
- Returning home only to find that we had actually arrived in a strange, parallel kingdom called Tavania!
- Every time my mother has to return to Gwildor, her home kingdom.
- The death of my father, at the hands of the White Knight of Forton.

Tom's Belt

Tom's Shield

Elenna grew up in the southwest of Avantia. Her parents died when she was a baby, after a fire swept through their village. Her uncle, Leo, was able to rescue baby Elenna, and he raised her ever since that day. A fisherman, Leo taught her how to fish, and how to sail a boat — thinking that, in the future, she would grow up and take over from him. But one day, when times were hard, Elenna had to go hunting in the Forest of Fear. Doing this made her fall foul of Avantia's guards, and she fled. Luckily, this was at the same time as a heroic young boy was setting off on his first Beast Quest. The young boy (Tom) helped her evade capture — and suddenly, Elenna's future as a fisherwoman was changed forever... Now, she would be an Avantian heroine, travelling to every corner of the kingdom on Beast Quests! Tom may have the tokens, but Elenna has the guile.

ELENNA

AGE:	13
POWER:	56
MAGIC LEVEL:	91
FEAR FACTOR:	68

In the future, she will put her skills to use, teaching Avantian cadets how to be elite archers, as well as to survive in the wild.

Actually, when you think about it, I'm much braver than Tom — because I have to face down danger without magical powers!

BEST MOMENTS:

- Meeting Tom for the first time in the Forest of Fear — if I hadn't been there, I'd have never gone on even one Beast Quest.
- Making it safely back to Avantia from Gorgonia — that place was horrible!
- When my bravery got through to Tom, breaking the Judge's spell that had bewitched him.

WORST MOMENTS:

- Having to wear a blue silk dress when the king celebrated our first completed Quest. In fact, any time I have to wear a dress is a "Worst Moment"!
- When Silver was left behind in Tavania… and, later, when my beloved wolf was turned into a terrifying Beast. It's hard to fight a monster when you know that monster is actually your loyal pet.
- When Mortaxe's magic made me turn on Tom — he has never told me what I said, or how I taunted him, and I never want to know!

TOM'S PIZZA SHIELD

TOM'S SHIELD PROTECTS HIM FROM NUMEROUS DANGERS. THIS PIZZA SHIELD IS THE ULTIMATE TRIBUTE TO ONE OF THE MOST VALUABLE ITEMS TOM TAKES ON A BEAST QUEST. MAKE PIZZA SHIELDS, FOR YOU AND A FRIEND...

YOUR INGREDIENTS (FOR TWO SHIELDS)

- Bread flour (250grams)
- Salt (1 teaspoon)
- Sugar (1 teaspoon)
- Yeast (3.5grams)
- Lukewarm water (160ml)
- Olive oil (1 tablespoon)
- Cheese
- Tomato sauce
- Toppings (This can be your choice — Mushrooms, pepperoni, peppers, courgettes, sweetcorn, jalapenos)

"Make sure you get the right mix of flavours — you don't want too many toppings. They'll fall off your shield!"

YOUR WEAPONS!

- Rolling pin
- Measuring spoons
- Scale
- Fork
- Sieve
- Bowl
- Baking tray
- Measuring cup or jug
- Pizza cutter or wheel
- Cloth
- Oven
- Oven-gloves (these are VERY important!)

1. Make sure your hands, and any work surfaces are CLEAN. Beast Quests might bc dirty work, but FOOD IS NOT!

2. Use measuring cup to measure all ingredients to the specified amounts, warm the water to approximately 37°.

3. Sieve the flower and salt into the bowl, making sure there are no lumps. Then make a well in the middle of the bowl.

4. Now mix the yeast, olive oil and sugar with the warm water in the jug. After about five minutes, the yeast should start to foam. After the yeast foams, pour it into the well in the bowl.

5. Mix the flour and the yeast, bringing flour in from all sides and swirling it with the liquid, making sure it does not get too sticky or too dry. USE ONE HAND — you'll need the other to add more flour if needed.

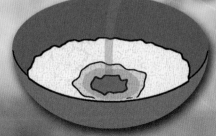

REMEMBER – THIS SHIELD IS NOT TO BE USED TO PROTECT YOU FROM DANGER. IT WILL ONLY HELP PROTECT YOU FROM HUNGER! ENJOY!

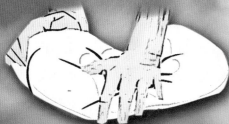

6. Knead the dough — you will need to be very strong. Stretch it out, then pull it back together, making sure that is soft and smooth and flexible.

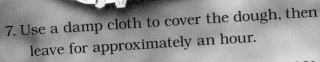

7. Use a damp cloth to cover the dough, then leave for approximately an hour.

8. Ask an adult to pre-heat the oven to 200°. This should take about ten minutes.

9. Take out the dough and knead some more, making sure that no air is trapped inside.

10. Sprinkle some flour on the work surface, then use the rolling pin to roll the dough into the right shape. Sprinkle more flour on the dough.

11. Once flat, use pizza cutter/wheel to cut the dough into the shape of the Shield!

12. Pour a tablespoon of oil onto the baking tray

13. Roll the Shield-shaped dough onto the baking tray

14. Use the fork to poke the dough, to make sure the air gets out.

15. By now, the oven should be heated. Put the dough in for five minutes, to make sure the crust is crisp.

16. After five minutes, USE THE OVEN GLOVES to take out the dough. Spread the tomato sauce on the base.

17. Sprinkle cheese over the tomato sauce.

18. Now... Choose Your Toppings! Add whatever you like over the cheese!

19. USE THE OVEN GLOVES to put pizza back in the oven.

20. Bake for 8-10 minutes, or until the crust has started to turn golden-brown.

21. Now that it's ready, USE THE OVEN GLOVES to take out your Pizza Shields!

Heroes carry shields to be safe. You should be safe too — always check with an adult before you start cooking, and ask them for help when using the oven, knives, or sharp equipment.

8-10 MINUTES ? THAT SOUNDS LIKE ENOUGH TIME TO HAVE AN ADVENTURE!

HISTORY OF MAGIC AND WIZARDRY IN AVANTIA

The kingdom of Avantia, as we know it, has existed for hundreds of years, stretching back even before the wars that saw the rise of the "first hero" Tanner, of whom you can read elsewhere in this Annual.

Before that era of chaos and destruction, in which Tanner and his three friends battled against the villains General Gor and Derthsin, the realm was an unassuming region, its people united not by kings and queens, but by trading alliances. In the east, towns like Forton (which would later be renamed Errinel) were home to farmers, who traded their harvested crops for precious metals mined in towns like Colton, in the northern mountains. It was a peaceful time.

Sounds like a boring time to me! It's a good thing that Wizards came into being at some point in this period of history, to liven things up! But typically, the people of Avantia were cowardly and cruel — the moment they got wind of there being special people in the realm, they banded together with flaming torches and silly ideas about dunking "the abnormal people" in the river. Because they were scared of magic…

Of course they were scared of magic! They had never seen anything like it before. It's not like nowadays, when the people have had hundreds of years to get used to there being Wizards in the kingdom. Unfortunately, we will never know who the first Avantians to be touched by magic were, because there were no scribes in any of the communities to record their history.

Probably because people back then were just too stupid to learn how to write!

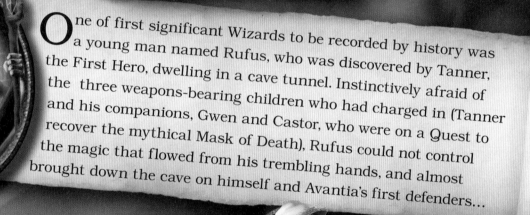

One of first significant Wizards to be recorded by history was a young man named Rufus, who was discovered by Tanner, the First Hero, dwelling in a cave tunnel. Instinctively afraid of the three weapons-bearing children who had charged in (Tanner and his companions, Gwen and Castor, who were on a Quest to recover the mythical Mask of Death), Rufus could not control the magic that flowed from his trembling hands, and almost brought down the cave on himself and Avantia's first defenders...

I wish he had done. If Tanner had perished in that cave, the great Evil warlord, Derthsin, would have prevailed, and darkness would have ruled this kingdom!

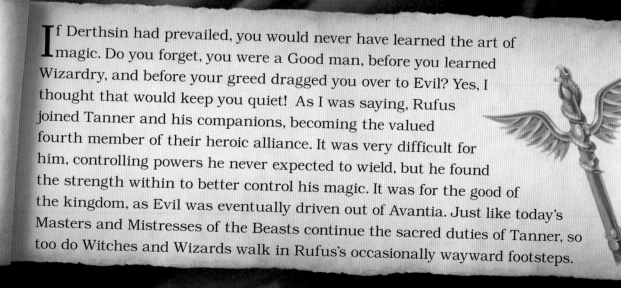

If Derthsin had prevailed, you would never have learned the art of magic. Do you forget, you were a Good man, before you learned Wizardry, and before your greed dragged you over to Evil? Yes, I thought that would keep you quiet! As I was saying, Rufus joined Tanner and his companions, becoming the valued fourth member of their heroic alliance. It was very difficult for him, controlling powers he never expected to wield, but he found the strength within to better control his magic. It was for the good of the kingdom, as Evil was eventually driven out of Avantia. Just like today's Masters and Mistresses of the Beasts continue the sacred duties of Tanner, so too do Witches and Wizards walk in Rufus's occasionally wayward footsteps.

WITCHES AND WIZARDS!

Most people in Avantia grow up hearing tales of Witches and Wizards, who cast spells that can turn people into frogs, and concoct potions that can either create or cure sicknesses. Very few actually get to meet one for real, though. One day, you might see a curious figure in long, colourful, flowing robes standing by the king if there's ever a Royal procession in your hometown, but that's as close as you will usually come. But after I met Tom, I found myself face-to-face with Wizards — both Good and Evil...

Our first, and greatest, mentor. Were it not for Aduro noticing the resemblance between me and my father, I would never have set off on my first Beast Quest. But there is still so much about him that I don't know, and he has promised to tell me all about his life and early adventures — just as soon as I get a break from saving all the kingdoms!

ADURO

AGE:	70
POWER:	276
MAGIC LEVEL:	192
FEAR FACTOR:	65

MALVEL

AGE:	57
POWER:	285
MAGIC LEVEL:	190
FEAR FACTOR:	100

I was so excited to find out Wizards were real, until I encountered this villain. Malvel seemed to never run out of new, evil ways to attack the kingdom — but Tom and I never stopped fighting him!

VELMAL

AGE: 59
POWER: 285
MAGIC LEVEL: 190
FEAR FACTOR: 100

I wonder if we've seen the last of this nefarious fiend, whose specialty was hideous poisons — he used one on my mother, and almost killed her!

She began as our enemy, thwarting us as we tried to save Good Beasts, but she is showing signs of turning to the side of Good. I'm just not sure we can trust her...

PETRA

AGE: 16
POWER: 120
MAGIC LEVEL: 120
FEAR FACTOR: 67

KAPRA

AGE: 40
POWER: 200
MAGIC LEVEL: 189
FEAR FACTOR: 50

...but it's understandable that Petra would grow up unpredictable, when her mother is as devious and conniving as Kapra! I believe that Kapra's evil influence on her daughter is broken for good!

TOP 5 SPELLS!

It takes a very long time to master spells and incantations. Apprentice Wizards spend many years learning them by heart, and days on end practicing how to correctly pronounce every single word – because one mistake can mean the difference between becoming invisible and becoming a toad! These are my five favourite spells – and the one I fear the most!

This spell is one of the most powerful, and can turn even the vastest of dragons invisible!

Clouds and cloaks, shadows and lies

Hide this creature from human eyes.

One of the most dangerous of spells, only to be used sparingly – a Master or Mistress of the Beasts must complete their Quest before the heat does damage to the ice!

Break the winter, snap the cold,

So the new Quest can unfold.

One of the spells I am still trying to master! If used correctly, any traitors in the palace will only be able to speak the truth – which will make it easier to protect His Majesty from harm!

Truth and honesty will rise,

Whenever the kingdom harbours spies.

I like this one – it will be perfect for making boring dinners more fun!

Sour the milk, ruin the taste,

Watch the diner flee with haste.

An ancient spell that can provide the ability to see in the dark. Be careful with this one, though – if you hesitate, or speak too softly, you could end up blind!

Through wide eyes is the best way

To see night like it is day.

AND A SPELL TO ALWAYS BEWARE...

Come, cruel magic of Malvel,

Fill these gauntlets with your spell.

Lure two Beasts to deadly battle,

Make them fight with tooth and claw

'Til one Beast lives and one draws breath no more.

This spell was used by Maximus, to infuse Tom's golden gauntlets with Dark Magic, so that he could bend Beasts to his will. He only managed to steal one of the gauntlets – but was still able to wreak havoc on Avantia with it!

POTIONS!

Most Apprentice Wizards grow up dreaming of being able to conjure balls of flame with just a few words, or waving their hands and making things disappear – it looks like so much fun, and it is. But being a Wizard also involves some messy, smelly work, as well – concocting potions is not always pleasant, but is sometimes necessary to undo Dark Poisons and other infections. Here are some of the most effective magical potions – but don't try to make at home, because you might never get the stench out!

THE GILDED ELIXIR

The only potion that will undo the evil effects of Lunar Blood, which can turn a Good Beast to bad. For this, you will need:

Starleaf from the Murmuring Peak; Water, from the lost City of Snakes; the red root of the Hidden Tree in the Dark Jungle; and Burnstone, which is very hard to find.

Sounds easy-peasy, doesn't it?!

To save a friend who has been infected with Velmal's poison, you will need to mix six special ingredients.

- Black Cactus
- Muro's jade ring
- The red jewel of the Golden Valley
- The chain of vines from the marshes
- A special white flower from the forests
- Vespick's wasp sting

You will also need to go to Kayonia, as that is where these ingredients can be found!

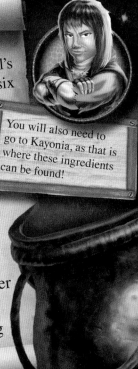

MAKE YOUR OWN WIZARD HAT

Every Wizard or Witch needs three things — knowledge of spells, ingredients for potions, and a fantastic hat! If you'd like to dress up like a magical protector of the kingdom, then study the steps and make your own Wizard hat!

- Cereal box card
- Ruler
- Scissors
- Sellotape
- Pencil
- Newspaper — at least three layers
- PVA Glue
- Paints — your choice of colour!

1 Use ruler to measure, then use pencil to mark a quarter-circle in the card. The radius should be approximately 50cm (draw a complete circle first, if this will help).

2 ASK AN ADULT to supervise as you use the scissors to cut out the quarter-circle.

3 Then roll it into a cone-shape. Make sure it fits your head, before using sellotape to secure it in place — you can't be a Wizard if your hat falls off when you're casting spells!

4 Lay another piece of card down flat on a table or work surface, and place the cone on top. (Can you see the hat beginning to take shape now?) Use the pencil to draw another circle around the cone — this will be the brim of your Wizard hat. (Don't worry if the edges are a little ragged — all the best Wizards' hats are messy!)

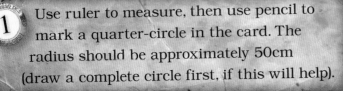

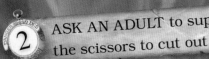
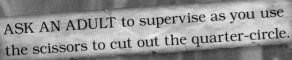

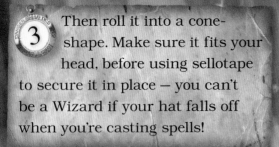

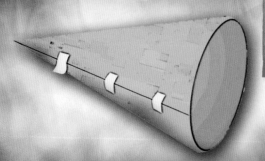

5 ASK AN ADULT to supervise as you cut out the circle you have just drawn. Draw another circle inside it, about 2cm inside, and cut that out too. CAREFULLY snip the scissors around the edge, making tabs.

6 Pull the tabs upwards, and then fit your cone around them, securing with the sellotape.

7 Now cover the whole hat with the three layers of newspaper, pasted on with the PVA glue. Leave it to dry.

8 Once it's dry, use the paints to paint your Wizard hat in any colour that you like!

CONGRATULATIONS – YOU NOW LOOK JUST LIKE A WIZARD. BUT BE SURE TO PRACTISE YOUR SPELLS BEFORE YOU START CASTING THEM AT VILLAINS!

DISCOVERING THE ICE DRAGON!

My father served Avantia as Master of the Beasts for many years before I assumed the role, and almost all of his exploits have been recorded by Avantia's scholars and historians. This is one of my favourite stories — an early adventure he had with the then-Prince Hugo…

Taladon clung on as the dragon flew through the air. The rushing wind stung his eyes, and threatened to rip his trembling fingers away from the green-and-red scales. But he had to hang on.

Prince Hugo needs me.

The dragon seemed unconcerned about its rider. It began to circle in sweeping arcs — a predator sizing up its prey. Shaking his long blond hair from his eyes, Taladon peered over the side of the Beast to scour the distant ground. His stomach dropped at the dizzying height.

There! He spotted the figure of Prince Hugo still sprawled on his front beside the embers of the campfire they had made, where he had been knocked to the ground by a flick of the Beast's tail. His Highness's golden plate-mail was stained with dry black earth, and his helmet lay some distance away.

Taladon winced as he remembered the moment he returned from collecting firewood in the Dead Forest, seeing the Beast ambush the young prince. The horrible, sickening thunk as Hugo's head hit the rock, the impact knocking him unconscious.

This expedition was supposed to have been a routine survival exercise for Taladon, to prepare him for the trials he would undergo in the future, when he would take on the title of Master of the Beasts, as predicted by Aduro, Wizard to Avantia's King Theo.

But thanks to the unexpected arrival of the dragon, it had turned into something far more deadly.

Get up! Taladon willed the prince. The Beast would not wait long before launching another attack. He felt a rush of relief as Hugo began to slowly drag his arms beneath his armoured chest. Shakily, the prince pushed himself up onto his feet.

The relief didn't last long. As if reacting to the movement, the Beast dived. Taladon had to press his body close to the leathery scales to avoid being falling to his death. The dragon's long body swayed back and forth propelling it faster and faster towards the jittery prince.

I have to do something.

Beneath Taladon, a rumbling, crackling sound grew deep in the dragon's throat. Its jaws opened, ready to blast deadly fire at Hugo.

"NO!" Taladon launched himself forward, tumbling down the neck and over the Beast's large green eyes. Blinded, it thrashed its jaws, and sprayed its blast in all directions — not fire, but ice. Prince Hugo dove aside, avoiding the freezing blast, looking up

in shock. "Taladon!" he called. "It's a Ghost Beast — that's Blaze the Ice Dragon!"

The Beast blinked out of sight. Taladon fell straight through the semi-transparent form, spinning wildly. He caught flashing glimpses of the ground as it whirled up to slam into him.

There was only one thing for it. He reached for the knapsack flapping from his belt, digging desperately inside, his heart hammering. At last he felt the soft brush of the eagle feather, given to him by Arcta. He withdrew it from the sack and raised it above his head. Only yards from the ground, Taladon slowed, as if an invisible hand had reached down from the sky and grabbed him by the collar. He slowed to a gentle glide, bending his legs and landing in a roll beside Hugo.

The pale prince put a hand on his shoulder. "Thank you for saving me." Taladon pointed up at the Ice Dragon, who had changed back to its flesh-and-blood form and was circling once more.

There was no time to lose. Taladon hurried to the pile of logs he had dropped when he began battling Blaze. Now, he kicked them onto the campfire, the flames rising higher and sending a wave of heat into his face. Hugo hurried over, locking arms with Taladon, clearly understanding his plan. Together, they turned, backs to the fire, staring up at Blaze.

Above, the Beast tucked in its wings and plummeted straight towards them. The shape of the Ice Dragon grew and grew, until it blocked out the harsh sun of the Forbidden Land.

"Hold..." said Taladon to the prince, through clenched teeth. The Beast was close enough for Taladon to stare into his slitted eyes. "Hold!"

The dragon's jaws opened wide, displaying green dagger-like teeth. "Now!"

They jumped in opposite directions. Blaze crashed straight into the fierce flames of the campfire, sending burning splints of wood flying. Howling with pain and rage it twisted sideways, over and over, desperately trying to smother its burning scales on the black earth.

"Poor creature," said Taladon, as the dragon weakly retreated towards the cover of the Dead Forest, disappearing in the dense, black undergrowth.

"You are right to pity him," replied Prince Hugo. "But never forget, Blaze is evil — he has no soul to redeem."

Taladon felt his fists clench with determination. "While there's blood in my veins," he said, "Blaze will never cross the Forbidden Land into Avantia!"

DRAW YOUR OWN BEAST

Tom and Elenna have been on almost one hundred Quests, but that doesn't mean they have seen every type of Beast — they know there are always surprises awaiting them in the future. Help them stay prepared by thinking of a Beast they haven't faced yet. Is it a land- or a sea-Beast? Does it patrol the skies? Is its home a fiery cavern, or an icy cave? What about a forest, a jungle, or a desert? You must help Tom and Elenna think of all the possible dangers, so that Avantia's heroes are well-prepared for this challenge — just in case they come face-to-face with it in the future...

What are the elements of a Beast that you would LEAST like to face? Only by expecting the worst of dangers can Tom and Elenna be prepared for them.

DANGERS COULD INCLUDE:

- Fiery breath
- Mandible jaws
- Long, forked tongue (possibly venomous)
- Vicious claws
- Cruel talons
- Spiked tails
- Massive height
- Vast width
- Shell
- Body made of scales, or a rough hide
- Spikes
- Horns
- Wings
- Multiple heads

Don't forget, some Beasts bear weapons, making them extra dangerous. What might your Beast use to attack his enemies? A long whip, like Arax and Soltra? Maybe a net and trident like Hecton? What about a deadly scythe, like Mortaxe? Does your Beast have smaller animals on leashes, like Ravira, to prevent heroes from getting too close?

I know that thinking of the most terrifying Beast possible isn't always fun, but it's sometimes necessary — only by thinking of the worst, can we be ready for it. So don't hold back — come up with the most frightening Beast you can imagine!

A BATTLE OF WITS

IT'S NOT JUST STRENGTH AND BRAVERY THAT TOM NEEDS ON A BEAST QUEST – SOMETIMES, HE MUST THINK HIS WAY OUT OF DANGER.

CAN YOU USE YOUR BEAST QUEST KNOWLEDGE TO ANSWER THE CLUES BELOW? WHEN YOU'VE COMPLETED THE GRID, REARRANGE THE LETTERS IN THE SHADED SQUARES TO REVEAL THE NAME OF A TERRIBLE KINGDOM, WHERE MALVEL TURNED PEOPLE AND INNOCENT CREATURES INTO BEASTS – INCLUDING ELENNA'S WOLF, SILVER!

ACROSS

1. Avantia's first Beast (6)
3. Gwildor's Master of the Sea (5)
5. Shape-shifting Beast, who once pretended to be Elenna (4)
6. The "Moon-Wolf" (4)
8. This Beast is called "The Walking Mountain" (4)
10. The first Beast Tom faced (5)
12. The Beast who gave Tom his enchanted bell token (6)
14. The Beast also known as the "Clawed Roar"
16. This Beast's whip can steal your soul (4)
18. _____ the Arctic Warrior (5)
19. Terrifying area of The Forbidden Land, "The ____ Jungle" (4)
20. Neighbouring kingdom where young Beasts are trained to become mighty protectors (4)

DOWN

1. Tom's home kingdom (7)
2. Grashkor guards the "Chamber of____" (4)
3. The Two-Headed Demon is called 'Kragos and_____" (6)
4. The Ghost-Beast known as the "Cave Troll"?
7. Mountain town in Gwildor (4)
9. Evil Sorceress and cohort of Sanpao (5)
11. The Beast who lives in the Stonewin Volcano (4)
13. The Swamp Man (4)
15. Gorgonian "Winged Stallion" (4)
17. The ___ Jewel allows Tom to communicate with Beasts (3)

THE KINGDOM OF :  _____

A BATTLE OF WITS

THE JUDGE HAS HIDDEN THE NAMES OF HEROES AND VILLAINS INSIDE THE FIENDISH GRID BELOW. YOU MUST HELP TOM FIND THEM ALL. EACH WORD COULD BE UP, DOWN, LEFT, RIGHT OR DIAGONAL. SOME WORDS WILL SHARE THE SAME LETTERS, AND SOME HAVE BEEN FLIPPED BACKWARDS!

A	D	F	K	S	L	E	V	L	A	M	S	K	V	A
S	F	H	E	F	A	Q	J	E	C	B	Q	H	M	D
R	R	J	G	S	T	O	R	M	L	R	W	R	K	A
M	E	D	L	Y	D	A	P	L	D	M	O	A	D	L
O	Y	A	F	P	A	P	O	O	H	S	A	T	T	T
T	A	L	A	D	O	N	O	Q	R	A	K	L	Y	E
L	Z	X	R	O	M	A	N	I	E	U	D	Y	A	C
K	Q	A	P	A	P	S	T	A	N	G	D	P	R	N
E	A	P	E	O	W	Q	T	G	A	V	F	A	P	A
N	A	E	X	R	O	A	T	B	N	Q	M	O	D	D
S	E	T	H	R	I	N	A	T	A	H	C	S	F	D
A	E	R	B	K	I	N	G	H	U	G	O	I	T	A
S	I	A	T	H	Q	E	C	T	H	K	P	D	G	E
H	K	D	T	H	C	L	V	E	V	S	E	H	H	H
A	D	J	U	D	G	E	T	S	I	L	V	E	R	Y

SHADE IN EACH WORD AS YOU FIND IT. THE LETTERS IN THE ORANGE BOXES WILL REVEAL THE NAME OF THE HERO TOM NEEDS TO HELP HIM ON THIS QUEST...

WORDS TO FIND:

ADURO	KENSA	ROMAINE	STORM
DALTEC	KING HUGO	SANPAO	TALADON
ELENNA	MALVEL	SETH	TOM
FREYA	MARC	SETHRINA	VELMAL
JUDGE	PETRA	SILVER	

31

Beast Battle!

One place I never like to enter is Mortaxe's Arena. All through Avantian History, the Skeleton Warrior has drawn Beasts to his lair and made them fight each other to the death. When one Beast fights another, the whole kingdom is at risk from the carnage they can cause. But now, Mortaxe is playing host to Maximus, the son of Malvel. The cunning young Wizard has brought with him Koron, the Jaws of Death, and is challenging me to a duel. Study the profile of Koron, then help me choose the best opponent for this Beast Battle...

STRENGTH

The lion-Beast's tail is quick and deadly, able to keep most of his foes at a distance. It is also tinged with a deadly poison. If he strikes you with it, your body could dissolve!

The tail might be deadly, but it is also unpredictable. If a hero can turn it against the Beast, they have a chance to strike a deadly wound of their own!

WEAKNESS

Koron's ferocious teeth are not only razor-sharp, they also drip with the same deadly poison as his tail.

STRENGTH

AGE:	389
POWER:	270
MAGIC LEVEL:	167
FRIGHT FACTOR:	94

KORON

TAGUS

AGE:	406
POWER:	73
MAGIC LEVEL:	114
FRIGHT FACTOR:	58

STRENGTH

In addition to being one of the quickest Beasts, Tagus is also one of the few that carries a weapon. He wields his rusty sword with immense skill, and could keep Koron at a safe distance.

WEAKNESS

As brave as he is, Tagus would be significantly smaller than Koron. If the Evil Beast was able to close the distance and get Tagus on the ground, he could keep him there.

AMICTUS

AGE:	288
POWER:	199
MAGIC LEVEL:	189
FRIGHT FACTOR:	92

STRENGTH

In the close confines of her jungle, Amictus can camouflage herself extremely well. You won't know she's attacking until it's too late!

WEAKNESS

But if her first attacks are not successful, Amictus's long, awkward legs make her vulnerable when fighting a skilled opponent...

RAFFKOR

AGE:	4
POWER:	223
MAGIC LEVEL:	181
FRIGHT FACTOR:	85

STRENGTH

Against Koron, Raffkor would have a significant size advantage. If he could pin the Evil Beast onto the ground, he could force him to submit.

WEAKNESS

Raffkor is a very young Beast, and can occasionally lose his temper — if he does this, he can make a mistake, and Koron will have the chance to launch a deadly counter-attack.

All three of these Beasts would fight Koron with courage, doing their best to keep the kingdom safe from Evil. But who do YOU think I should choose?

I think Tom should choose_____

Avantia

THE ICY PLAINS

THE PIT OF FIRE

MALVEL'S MAZE

STONEWIN VOLCANO

THE DEAD VALLEY

THE DEAD JUNGLE

THE DARKWOOD

ERRINEL

THE DARK JUNGLE

THE CITY

KING HUGO'S PALACE

GRASSY PLAINS

THE CENTRAL PLAINS

THE WINDING RIVER

SPINDREL

THE NORTHERN MOUNTAINS

THE FOREST OF FEAR

THE RUBY DESERT

WESTERN OCEAN

AVANTIA

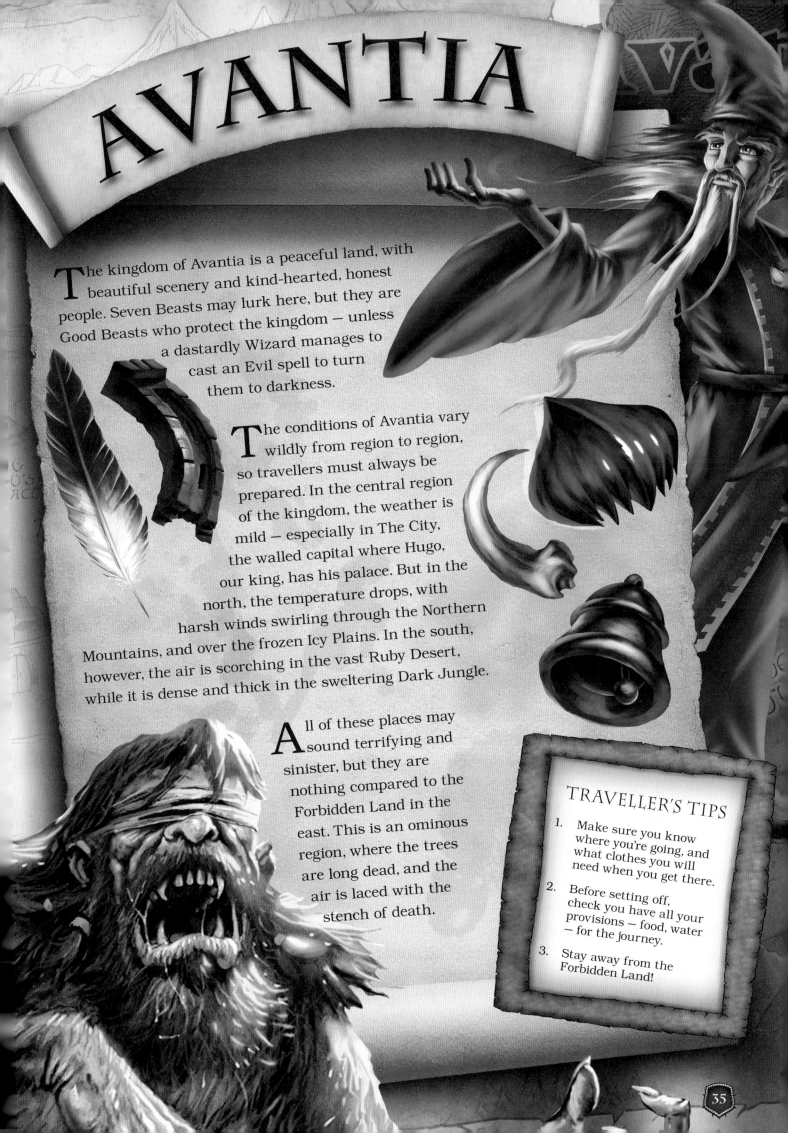

The kingdom of Avantia is a peaceful land, with beautiful scenery and kind-hearted, honest people. Seven Beasts may lurk here, but they are Good Beasts who protect the kingdom — unless a dastardly Wizard manages to cast an Evil spell to turn them to darkness.

The conditions of Avantia vary wildly from region to region, so travellers must always be prepared. In the central region of the kingdom, the weather is mild — especially in The City, the walled capital where Hugo, our king, has his palace. But in the north, the temperature drops, with harsh winds swirling through the Northern Mountains, and over the frozen Icy Plains. In the south, however, the air is scorching in the vast Ruby Desert, while it is dense and thick in the sweltering Dark Jungle.

All of these places may sound terrifying and sinister, but they are nothing compared to the Forbidden Land in the east. This is an ominous region, where the trees are long dead, and the air is laced with the stench of death.

TRAVELLER'S TIPS

1. Make sure you know where you're going, and what clothes you will need when you get there.
2. Before setting off, check you have all your provisions — food, water — for the journey.
3. Stay away from the Forbidden Land!

KING HUGO

AGE: 56
POWER: 243
MAGIC LEVEL: 40
FEAR FACTOR: 70

We all know that Avantia needs heroes, but just as important is having a strong leader, who can give hope to the people, even in the darkest of times. Whenever our kingdom is attacked by enemies, one thing on which Avantians can always rely is the knowledge that their king, Hugo, will never surrender...

THE WARRIOR KING

Before he was king, the young Prince Hugo was the second son of King Theo. Brave and honourable, Theo was beloved by his people, who nicknamed him "Soldier King" — an affectionate label for a ruler whose preferred position in battle was on the front line, with a weapon in hand.

As second son, Hugo was destined for a life without responsibility. All of the leadership duties were to fall on to the shoulders of his older brother, Angelo, who was a skilled and astute fighter. Avantia was in good hands, and so Hugo grew into a fun-loving, carefree young man who did not take his sword-fighting practice all that seriously — because he didn't have to!

But everything changed, one fateful day. More than thirty years before Tom set off on his very first Quest, wicked Malvel stirred rebellion in the north, by deceiving mining communities into believing that the king was preserving all the wealth for himself and his family. The Dark Wizard's aim was to rip the kingdom's alliances apart, so that the armies of Tangala — a kingdom to the south — would have an easier time conquering Avantia. Prince Angelo led the Avantian army into battle, but his forces were made up of soldiers who lived and trained in The City — they were not used to the unforgiving cold of the Northern Mountains, nor the Icy Plains. The rebels won an easy victory — and Prince Angelo did not make it home alive.

Now, Hugo was first in line to the throne. If he thought that he would have some time to prepare, to get used to what his duties would be when he became king, he was wrong. His father never recovered from the loss of his first son, and would soon die of a broken heart. Prince Hugo was now King Hugo, and — even though he did not feel ready for the responsibility — he sought the advice of Avantia's Wizard. Aduro promised to guide the new king, and became his most trusted advisor as His Majesty rose to the occasion, marshalling his armies astutely and protecting Avantia's borders from enemies in the north and the south, as well as pirates who tried to invade from the west.

His father may have been the "Soldier King" — but to his people, Hugo will always be known as "Warrior King".

LOST IN TAVANIA!

You've read about how my Quest in Tavania ended — Elenna and I captured Malvel, and dragged him through a portal back to Avantia... but Silver and my mother could not make it through in time. What you haven't read about is the story that happened after that. I didn't know for a long time, until my after mother had safely returned from Tavania, when she sat me down to tell me her story...

I stood in the doorway of the throne room, swinging my sword with all my strength — strength that was fast-fading because we had already been fighting hard against the numerous soldiers who had been corrupted by Malvel. I heard Elenna's cry behind me, and I knew that the portal back to Avantia was closing. I wanted so desperately to make it through, because I could not bear to be parted from my son again — but I also knew I could not take my eyes off the soldiers. They were trying their best to slip past me, to make it to the portal and pull Malvel back from the kingdom where he would face justice. Or maybe, they would escape into Avantia themselves, where they would run wild — new threats to Tom's kingdom. Whatever their plans were, I knew they were not good plans — and that only I was standing in their way now.

My sword struck armour with dull crunches and echoing clangs, but beneath the reverberations of combat, I heard the rushing sound of the portal closing. I heard an anguished cry as Silver put his body between his mistress and an evil soldier making one last attempt to attack her. Then the heavy silence left behind when the portal closed.

My son had disappeared into another world.

In front of me, Malvel's soldiers hesitated, lowering their weapons as they exchanged confused glances. Now that their evil master had been taken, they had no one to fight for. But in trying to help the Dark Wizard take the kingdom for himself, they were now enemies of Tavania — which meant the only thing they had left to fight for was their freedom, to stay out of the palace dungeons.

This meant, they could prove to be very dangerous opponents.

"Oradu," I said, turning to Tavania's Good Wizard, who was breathless after having opened the portal.

"Yes, Mistress Freya?" he said, adjusting his long, purple robe.

"Have you recovered from sending my son and his best friend back to Avantia?" I asked him.

"I do believe my strength is returning to me," he replied.

I pointed the tip of my sword at the traitorous soldiers. "Then might you turn that strength on the enemies of your kingdom, my good Sorcerer?"

Oradu's beard twitched as he gave a grim smile, his crinkly eyes twinkling. "With pleasure," he said. Then he raised his hands, which quickly became encased in balls of swirling blue flame. He aimed the blue flame at the soldiers, who turned tail and ran as fast as they could out of the throne room, and out into the courtyard. The soldiers thought they were safe, but they were wrong. Waiting for them outside were the Beasts of Tavania!

The fearsome protectors unleashed their rage on the treacherous soldiers, sending them scurrying in all directions. But there was nowhere for the soldiers to run — if they didn't run into the path of a Beast, they found themselves heading towards the blades wielded by the honourable soldiers I was leading out of the throne room in a deadly charge.

Even Silver got in on the act. Elenna's wolf came bounding out into the courtyard, his fur spiked with rage, his teeth bared in a deadly snarl. He snapped his jaws at any man who tried to subdue him, keeping them at bay.

After Dalaton and his men re-joined the fight, it did not take long for the forces of Good to prevail. While Tavania's new hero rounded up Malvel's minions, to be taken to the dungeons, the Wizard Oradu approached me. His face was grave, and apologetic.

"Forgive me," he said. "It was not my intention that you be separated from your son."

My heart was breaking, but I shook my head and told him, "I'm not angry at you. Malvel could not be allowed to escape again. You were protecting your kingdom, as a Good Wizard should do."

"Nevertheless," said Oradu, "you have my word, I shall work hard to re-establish a connection with Avantia. I will get you back to Tom — it will just… take some time."

Before I could answer, Silver gave a howl of distress and went scampering across the courtyard, his long claws clattering on the stone.

"No, Silver," I called. "Come back!"

But the wolf didn't listen to me. One or two of the soldiers tried to restrain him, but Silver was too crafty, weaving in and out of their legs. He was past the broken city walls in a flash of grey. I knew that he was unfamiliar with Tavania, and could very easily get lost — but I also knew that, if I didn't find him soon, I might never find him again.

And there was no way I was going to return to Avantia without bringing Elenna's wolf with me.

On the other side of the walls, Tavania's city gave way to a dense forest. I was so tired, my legs could barely keep me upright, but I kept running, letting my eyes drop to the soft earth, keeping track of Silver's pawprints, which led me deep into the woods.

I held my sword high, cautious and wary as I continued stepping forward. I whistled, hoping to catch Silver's attention, but the sound was quickly swallowed up by the trees, silence falling over the forest like a heavy cloak.

"Silver!" I hissed.

Whoosh!

With the thick treetops blocking out much of the sun, the blade that swiped towards me did not shine or glint — I barely saw it in time to duck, and felt a pinch at my scalp as the blade sliced off a lock of my hair. With a growl, I lashed out my sword, slamming the flat of the blade into the knee of my attacker — a soldier of Malvel's, who had sprung from behind a tree.

The villain collapsed to his knees and tried to scramble clear, but I was already on my feet and stamping my boot down onto the tail of his cloak, pinning him to the ground. Before he could move, I sank to the ground, placing my knees on his back and my free hand on his neck.

"It's over," I told him. "Whatever riches your Wizard master promised you, he can't deliver them. He's gone from this kingdom."

The soldier struggled, whimpering as he tried to push me off. But then he gave up, his whole body going slack.

I was about to drag him to his feet, when I heard a crunching sound behind me. Footsteps on the forest floor…

I reacted too late.

I was Gwildor's Mistress of the Beasts, but I was far from my home kingdom — and I was utterly exhausted from the earlier battle. Because of this, the second treacherous soldier was able to have a blade to my throat before I could react.

I froze, letting my sword fall to the ground, as the soldier snarled at me, "Get up!"

I did as commanded, taking deep breaths as I thought furiously to come up with a way out of this. But I was unarmed, and facing two sword-wielding soldiers now that the first had got to his feet and picked up my weapon. He aimed the blade at me.

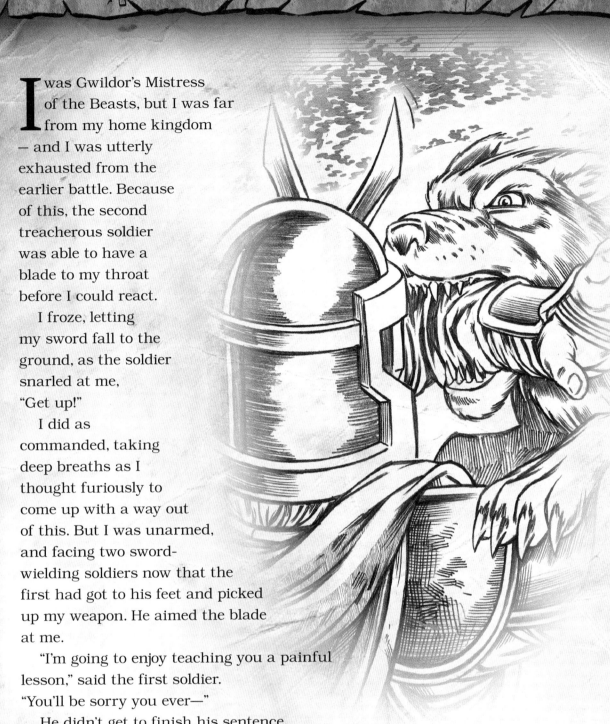

"I'm going to enjoy teaching you a painful lesson," said the first soldier. "You'll be sorry you ever—"

He didn't get to finish his sentence.

He was taken to the ground by a flying ball of grey fur. The second soldier made to intervene, but my saviour sank his teeth into his arm.

It was Silver!

Soon, the two soldiers had dropped their weapons, and were running for their lives. Silver bound after them long enough to make sure they were not going to regroup and come back — then he turned and padded up to me. I bent down to give him a grateful hug.

"You saved me, Silver," I gasped.

But then, all the energy in the wolf seemed to seep out of him, as he looked up at me with wide, sad eyes, before turning his face to the treetops and sending a heartbroken howl up towards the sky. I hugged him tighter.

"Don't you worry, boy," I said, doing my best to sound assured, determined. "I'll get you back to your mistress. Whatever it takes, we will return to Avantia — I swear it!"

GORGONIA

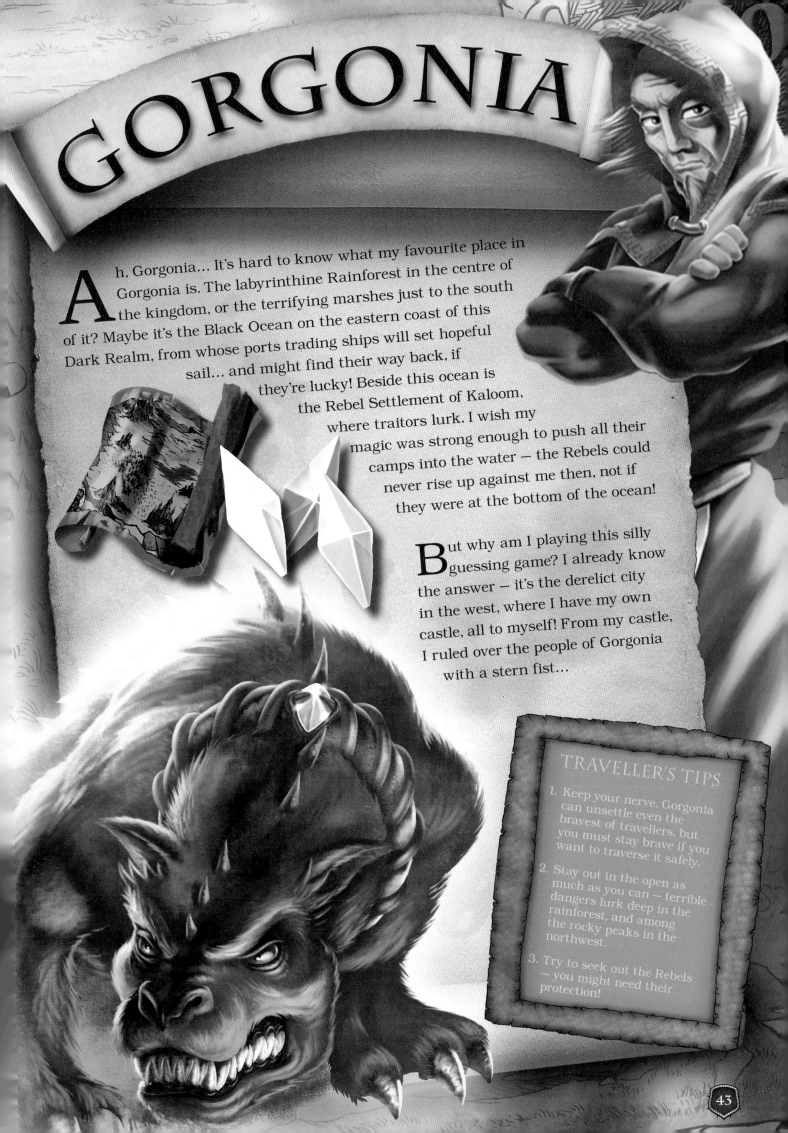

Ah, Gorgonia... It's hard to know what my favourite place in Gorgonia is. The labyrinthine Rainforest in the centre of the kingdom, or the terrifying marshes just to the south of it? Maybe it's the Black Ocean on the eastern coast of this Dark Realm, from whose ports trading ships will set hopeful sail... and might find their way back, if they're lucky! Beside this ocean is the Rebel Settlement of Kaloom, where traitors lurk. I wish my magic was strong enough to push all their camps into the water — the Rebels could never rise up against me then, not if they were at the bottom of the ocean!

But why am I playing this silly guessing game? I already know the answer — it's the derelict city in the west, where I have my own castle, all to myself! From my castle, I ruled over the people of Gorgonia with a stern fist...

TRAVELLER'S TIPS

1. Keep your nerve. Gorgonia can unsettle even the bravest of travellers, but you must stay brave if you want to traverse it safely.

2. Stay out in the open as much as you can — terrible dangers lurk deep in the rainforest, and among the rocky peaks in the northwest.

3. Try to seek out the Rebels — you might need their protection!

BEASTS OF THE SEA!

EVERY BEAST QUEST IS DANGEROUS, BUT THE QUESTS AT SEA ARE THE MOST DANGEROUS - AND THE MOST TERRIFYING! ON THESE QUESTS, WE FACE DANGER BEFORE WE HAVE EVEN GOT NEAR THE BEASTS (THE SURFACE OF THE SEA CAN BE VERY TREACHEROUS), AND WHEN WE DO FACE DOWN THE MASSIVE CREATURES, WE ARE USUALLY DOING SO ON A RAFT, OR IN A DINGHY. TRUST ME - IT'S TOUGH TO SWING A SWORD WHEN YOU DON'T HAVE YOUR BALANCE - AND ONE WRONG STEP COULD PLUNGE YOU INTO A WATERY GRAVE!

ZEPHA

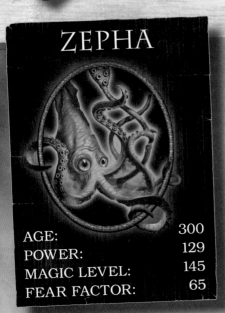

AGE:	300
POWER:	129
MAGIC LEVEL:	145
FEAR FACTOR:	65

WEAKNESS

Very few — but any warrior who gets past the tentacles has a good shot at wounding him between or above the eyes, where Zepha is very vulnerable!

STRENGTH

If his massive tentacles don't squeeze all the air from your body, his ink can blind you.

WEAKNESS

Those legs might be long, but they do not provide cover for Krabb's back. The Good Beast is very vulnerable to attacks from above.

KRABB

AGE:	261
POWER:	190
MAGIC LEVEL:	184
FEAR FACTOR:	88

STRENGTH

His eight long, spindly legs can keep attackers at a distance. His pincers are sharp enough to cut through sharks!

BALISK

AGE: 278
POWER: 237
MAGIC LEVEL: 171
FEAR FACTOR: 90

STRENGTH

Balisk may be a huge snake, but his fins make him a deceptively quick swimmer. He can also split his body in two, to launch dual attacks on his enemies!

WEAKNESS

If you can trick Balisk's two halves into colliding into each other, the wicked Beast will be at your mercy!

STRENGTH

Good luck trying to get close to this monstrous shark — even if you manage to avoid his many rows of vicious teeth, his serrated bone fins can still chop you into pieces!

SOLAK

AGE: 399
POWER: 256
MAGIC LEVEL: 134
FEAR FACTOR: 89

WEAKNESS

The only way I could defeat Solak was to blow him up from inside his own body. But I could only do that because I had the Blue Lightning Token — which is very rare!

HOW TO SURVIVE AT SEA

No one wants to get lost or stranded at sea, but there are some things you can do to ensure you survive.

1. Look for flotsam, or driftwood. You can make a raft out of anything.

2. Always have fresh drinking water with you — seawater will not help with dehydration!

3. If you can't locate a raft, and you're stranded in water, avoid hypothermia by holding your knees to your chest. This will help you retain as much body heat as possible while you await a rescue!

4. Hopefully, you won't have to face any sharks but, if you do, you will want to have a sword with you. Using the flat of the blade to bash them on the nose is the best chance you have of keeping them at bay!

5. Most importantly of all — always practice your swimming whenever you can. It could end up saving your life!

BEAST QUEST QUIZ!

When they're not on a Beast Quest, Tom and Elenna make an effort to study up on all things Beastly, because it's not just bravery and toughness that they need to complete a Beast Quest — knowledge is very useful, too. Test YOUR knowledge of their adventures, and the Beasts they have faced.

QUESTION #1
Who was the first Beast Tom ever faced?

(A.) Ferno
(B.) Sepron
(C.) Arcta

QUESTION #2
Where did Malvel hide the stolen golden helmet, and which terrifying Beast guarded it?

(A.) Claw, in the Dark Jungle
(B.) Arachnid, in Spindrel
(C.) Zepha, in the Western Ocean

QUESTION #3
What is the biggest danger when facing Soltra the Stone Charmer?

(A.) That she will strangle you with her whip
(B.) That she will turn you to stone
(C.) That she will drown you in the marsh

QUESTION #4
What is the surest way for a Quester to prevail against Kragos and Kildor?

(A.) Making their two heads fight each other
(B.) Chopping off their horns to weaken them
(C.) Setting their fur on fire

QUESTION #5
Who is the final Beast to defeat on The Warrior's Road?

- A. Skurik
- B. Targro
- C. Koba

QUESTION #6
What is the name of the monstrous tree lurking in the Kayonian forests?

- A. Muro
- B. Terra
- C. Fang

QUESTION #7
From whom did Tagus acquire his sword?

- A. Another Beast
- B. A former Master of the Beasts
- C. A bounty hunter looking to capture the Horse-Man

QUESTION #8
How many heads does Narga the Sea Monster have?

- A. Six
- B. Nine
- C. Twelve

QUESTION #9
Which Beast patrols Tavania's Southern River?

- A. Hellion
- B. Ellik
- C. Krestor

QUESTION #10
What is the name of the Beast who can consume you in her foul cloak, after conjuring an eerie light to lure you into the forest?

- A. Cornix
- B. Ravira
- C. Soltra

GUESS THE IMPOSTOR

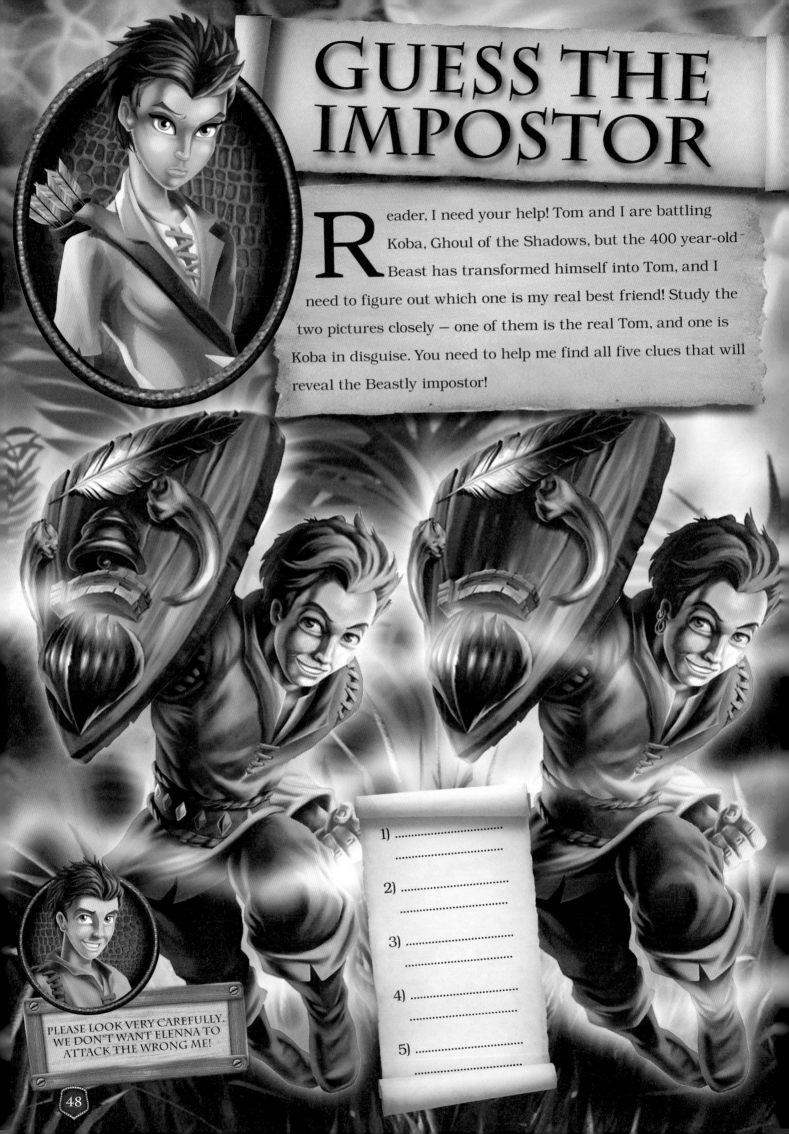

Reader, I need your help! Tom and I are battling Koba, Ghoul of the Shadows, but the 400 year-old Beast has transformed himself into Tom, and I need to figure out which one is my real best friend! Study the two pictures closely — one of them is the real Tom, and one is Koba in disguise. You need to help me find all five clues that will reveal the Beastly impostor!

PLEASE LOOK VERY CAREFULLY. WE DON'T WANT ELENNA TO ATTACK THE WRONG ME!

1) ....
....

2) ....
....

3) ....
....

4) ....
....

5) ....
....

SURVIVING A QUEST!

On a Beast Quest, you will often find yourself in the wilderness, far from the nearest town. If that happens, you will need to find food and water where you can. Here is a brief introduction to surviving the non-Beastly parts of a Quest, so that you can stay safe and energised, ready to tackle the next monstrous challenge!

IF LOST IN WOODLAND:

Plants don't always look very tasty, but look closer and you might see nuts and berries. But be careful — some will be poisonous! Before you set off on your Quest, you should study up and make yourself familiar with the good and bad foods you'll find in the woods. The safer option is to chew long grass for its juice (just remember to spit it out!).

THE FOREST OF FEAR

IF LOST IN THE DESERT:

Cactus plants might be painfully spiky, but they could come to your rescue in a desert. Check any nearby cacti for fruit that might be growing — all cacti fruits are edible, even if they're not especially tasty! SAFETY TIP: If you are in the desert without water, don't eat until you've found some. Your body will use up precious water trying to digest the food, and you will be further dehydrated!

THE RUBY DESERT

IF STRANDED IN THE MOUNTAINS:

Before climbing, you should stash an extra set of clothing in your backpack, as it can get cold at altitude. If you have to sleep up in the mountains, DO NOT sleep with your head angled downhill, as this will send your blood flowing in completely the wrong direction!

THE NORTHERN MOUNTAINS

TRUSTY COMPANIONS

TOM AND I MUST CONSTANTLY RELY ON OUR ANIMAL COMPANIONS TO HELP US ON OUR QUESTS. WHETHER IT'S HORSES CARRYING US VAST DISTANCES AT GREAT SPEED, OR BRAVE WOLVES WARDING OFF POTENTIAL ATTACKERS, THESE ANIMALS HAVE ALL PLAYED VITAL ROLES IN OUR SUCCESSES!

STORM

AGE:	15
POWER:	200
MAGIC LEVEL:	89
FEAR FACTOR:	50

Storm was already something of an Avantian legend, having won the annual City Derby — the most popular horse race event in the kingdom. Aduro told me that, before I arrived on my first Quest, Storm rejected all but the most special and skilled of riders, and was so jumpy that he was almost sent away from the City. It was the Wizard who saw Destiny in the black stallion, and advised His Majesty to keep Storm in the stables until his "true master" came. I am VERY relieved that Aduro was so wise back then, as Storm is as loyal a friend as I could hope for!

Silver roamed wild in the forests for many years — a real Lone Wolf. It was only by chance that we met, one day when I was very young. I got lost in the woods, and couldn't walk because I had badly injured my ankle — it was a kind, grey wolf who let me climb onto his back so that he could walk me safely back to my uncle, Leo. We've been friends ever since!

SILVER

AGE:	35
POWER:	147
MAGIC LEVEL:	34
FEAR FACTOR:	60

FLEETFOOT

Fleetfoot was my father's trusty horse, who was one of the fastest steeds I ever saw run. He also had an intuitive understanding with Taladon, who rarely needed to tug the reins to get Fleetfoot to change course!

AGE: 30
POWER: 250
MAGIC LEVEL: 89
FEAR FACTOR: 50

TEMPEST

AGE: 12
POWER: 210
MAGIC LEVEL: 100
FEAR FACTOR: 28

When we travelled to Henkrall, we had to leave Storm and Silver behind. But this winged, purple stallion was a more than adequate replacement, and quickly became a loyal companion!

This shaggy, winged wolf was twice the size of Silver, but that never slowed him down. On the ground, or in the air, Spark moved at great speed!

SPARK

AGE: 14
POWER: 156
MAGIC LEVEL: 100
FEAR FACTOR: 38

GWILDOR

If you sail west from Avantia's Western Ocean, the vast body of water eventually becomes a more vibrant shade of blue. This is the sign that you have now crossed into the Gwildorian Ocean, which will take you to Avantia's neighbouring kingdom. This is my home.

Gwildor's ocean will take you to walls of high cliffs, and a lush beach beside a fishing village. From there, the kingdom is much like Avantia, only more colourful. The farmland in the centre of the kingdom is rich in crops, enough to feed the entire population, and horses and deer happily roam the beautiful Gwildorian Plains.

There are some ominous-looking places, too — particularly Freeshor, the arctic region in the northwest. It is covered in snow all year round, and dotted with thick towers of ice that seem to rise up and scratch the sky. It is home to people who must wear thick, fur cloaks to stay warm.

Wildor is a beautiful place, and it is my wish that Tom will one day return here for an extended visit, so that I can teach him about his Gwildorian heritage...

TRAVELLER'S TIPS

1. Shield your eyes when you first arrive in Gwildor. The sheer colour in this kingdom takes a while to get used to!

2. If you find yourself in Freeshor, keep an eye out for hibernating bears. They definitely do not like being woken up!

53

SAVING SPIROS

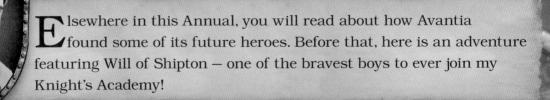

Elsewhere in this Annual, you will read about how Avantia found some of its future heroes. Before that, here is an adventure featuring Will of Shipton — one of the bravest boys to ever join my Knight's Academy!

Behold, the lost seventh Beast of Avantia!" roared Sanpao, stepping up onto the quarterdeck of his flying ship. He hoisted the small, rusty cage before the horde of jeering pirates. "Now, she is no better than a squawking parrot!"

Around Will, the pirates whistled and shouted. But he hardly heard them. From beneath his close-fitting hood, he gazed at the magically-shrunken Beast. He couldn't believe this pitiful creature was the same phoenix Tom had described to him before the mission. *Her eyes are emerald green, with the power of All-Sight. Her feathers burn brighter than the fires of Stonewin.*

Instead, the Beast's feathers were a rumpled mess, glowing faintly like dying embers. On its side a bloody gash oozed with the poison Sanpao had used to shrink her.

"And now, I shall finish her off!" shouted Sanpao, triumphantly.

Will felt a rush of panic as the Pirate King aimed his cutlass through the bars of the cage. He dug in his pocket for one of the magical tokens that Tom had given him — Balisk's claw — and flung it like a boomerang, straight at the startled Sanpao.

Immediately the pirates around him cried out, trying to grab him.

"He ain't no pirate!"

"Get the spy!"

Keeping low, Will charged out of the crowd, tracing the flight of the claw. Clang! Spiros's cage was knocked from Sanpao's grasp, rolling onto the deck. The cage door swung loose, and Will felt a surge of hope as the shrunken Beast flapped weakly from the cage and perched on the gunwale of the ship, watching him.

It's waiting for me, Will realised.

He charged towards Spiros. But before he could reach the Beast, a towering figure —

and a deadly, serrated cutlass — blocked
his path.

"Going somewhere?" said Sanpao,
grinning. "I expected Tom to plan a rescue
mission, but I didn't think he would send
one of his pitiful cadets."

"I'm a lieutenant now," Will retorted, as
Sanpao launched forwards with a flurry of
powerful blows.

Will scrambled backwards, reaching into
his cloak, where he had hidden the golden
trident given to him by Wizard Daltec. But he
was driven back and back, until his head hit the
hard wood of the mast behind him. The other pirates
gathered in a semi-circle around the two fighters, baying
for blood.

Will pranced aside as Sanpao viciously swung his cutlass, the
blade lodging into the mast, which spat splinters of wood onto the deck.
Sanpao shouted in rage as he tried to wrench it free. But it was stuck!

Will took his chance. He sprung off the deck, one foot landing on the
impaled cutlass blade, the other kicking into Sanpao's chest. As the Pirate King
staggered backwards, Will scampered up the mast, not looking back until he reached
the crow's nest at the top. He pulled himself up onto the viewing platform. He was safe…
for the moment. At this height, he could see right over the
side of the flying ship, and the seemingly endless
drop below. No way out.

A violent cheer carried up to Will from
the deck. He looked down to see Sanpao
clambering up the opposite mast, the cutlass
tucked back into his belt. "You think you
could escape me, boy?" he snarled.

This is it, thought Will. *My Quest is over.*

Then he caught sight of Spiros, flying alongside
the ship. Will knew what she wanted him to do.

He turned and bounded the length of the viewing platform. He kicked out as hard as
he could with his legs… and dived. He spread his arms to remain balanced in the air, the
wind whooshing in his ears. He fell past the side of ship. For a second he wondered if he
had made a mistake. Then, from below, he caught sight of a flash of red. *Spiros!*
The shrunken bird soared beneath him.

As Will plummeted side-by-side with Spiros, he pulled from his cloak the final token
he had been gifted for his Quest — Epos's magical phoenix talon, which had the ability
to heal wounds. He held it against the Spiros's infected cut. The shrinking poison
quickly seeped away, and the wound began to close. The Beast began to grow, each wing
spreading as wide as a ship's sail. Will gripped hold of the ruby red feathers, restored to
their full colour. Spiros beat her mighty wings, carrying them upwards, and safely away
from the ship. Will couldn't resist a look behind him at the raging pirates.

He gazed up at the crow's nest high above deck, and the shrinking figure of Sanpao
shaking his cutlass. *Even Tom would have been proud of that dive*, thought Will.

FIND THE CUP OF LIFE!

W e've just receieved some terrible news — Sanpao and his pirates have stolen the precious Cup of Life from Henry's forge and has hidden it somewhere in the Forest of Fear. Now that it has been taken out of the fire, its magic is beginning to slowly fade — if Tom doesn't find it soon, His Majesty King Hugo will lose his love for the kingdom! Can you help Tom find his way to the Cup before it is too late?

HOW TO PLAY

You will need a dice, plus a counter for each player. Place your counters on the start square, then roll the dice — whoever gets the highest number will go first. To play, roll the dice to see how many squares you can move. Good luck…

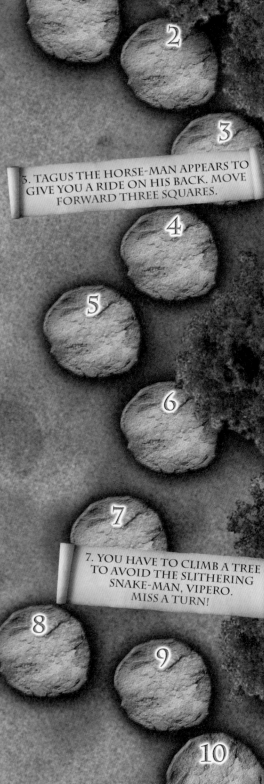

3. TAGUS THE HORSE-MAN APPEARS TO GIVE YOU A RIDE ON HIS BACK. MOVE FORWARD THREE SQUARES.

7. YOU HAVE TO CLIMB A TREE TO AVOID THE SLITHERING SNAKE-MAN, VIPERO. MISS A TURN!

10. BLOODBOAR RAMPAGES THROUGH THE FOREST, KNOCKING DOWN TREES. YOU'LL NEED TO FIND A NEW ROUTE THROUGH THE FOREST. GO BACK TWO SPACES.

FINISH

YOU REACH INTO THE TREE BRANCHES AND GRAB THE CUP OF LIFE. AS SOON AS YOU RETURN IT TO HENRY'S FORGE, AVANTIA WILL BE SAFE AGAIN!

44. YOU SEE THE CUP OF LIFE AT LAST, BUT SOLTRA APPEARS FROM BEHIND THE TREE! IF YOU LOOK AT THE BEAST, YOU'LL BE TURNED TO STONE. MISS A TURN

42. STEALTH THE GHOST PANTHER ATTACKS A PLAYER OF YOUR CHOICE. SEND THEM BACK TWO SPACES.

36. THE FLYING PIRATE SHIP APPEARS ABOVE THE TREES - SANPAO IS BACK. MISS A TURN WHILE YOU FIGHT OFF YOUR ENEMIES.

41. SANPAO AND HIS PIRATES FIRE ARROWS AT YOU FROM THE SKY. GO BACK ONE SPACE.

32. FREYA GIVES YOU SOME SWORD-FIGHTING ADVICE. GO FORWARD ONE SPACE.

30. CAREFUL - YOU'VE RUN INTO A SWARM OF STABIORS, WHICH MEANS THAT CRETA IS NEARBY. GO BACK TWO SPACES, AND FIND A NEW ROUTE THROUGH THE FOREST!

34. ALDROIM APPEARS OUT OF NOWHERE. THANKFULLY, STORM KICKS OUT HIS BACK-LEGS AND HITS THE SHAPE-SHIFTER IN THE HEAD. GO FORWARD THREE SPACES WHILE THE BEAST IS WOOZY.

27. DALTEC APPEARS IN THE FOREST, JUST BEFORE RAVIRA'S HOUNDS CAN ATTACK YOU. GO FORWARD TWO SPACES WHILE THE WIZARD PUTS THEM TO SLEEP WITH A MAGIC SPELL!

23. YOU COME TO A TREE HEAVY WITH FRUIT - YOU STOP TO EAT, AND FEEL STRONGER. MOVE FORWARD TWO SPACES!

20. STORM'S HEAVY HOOVES GIVE AWAY YOUR LOCATION TO CORNIX. MISS A TURN WHILE YOU HIDE FROM THE DEADLY TRICKSTER.

12. NASTY SETHRINA IS ABOUT TO SNEAK-ATTACK, BUT ELENNA FRIGHTENS HER OFF WITH A WARNING ARROW. GO FORWARD THREE SPACES!

19. ASK FERNO TO CARRY A PLAYER OF YOUR CHOICE BACK TO THE START.

TOOLS OF THE BEASTLY TRADE!

"May this boy have the strength of heart to save Avantia."

Those were the words uttered by Wizard Aduro, the day I set off on my very first Beast Quest. He had brought a sword and shield to my bedchamber, and handed them to me. I remember, the sword felt light and looked sharp, and was obviously going to be more useful to me than the poker that I had always used for practice back in Errinel.

That "practice" would serve me well on my Quests, for I was able to wield my blade with skill and precision when the time came. But swords would not be the only weapons I would use on my Quests — from time to time, I would have to fight with other tools. Some of them I was comfortable with, others felt clumsy and dangerous — but each of them has saved my skin at one time or another!

BALISK'S CLAW

Sometimes, you will have to fight up close with a blade — but other times, you can keep your enemies at bay with weapons like this. Be careful, though — if you don't throw with accuracy, not only will you miss your target, but you will lose your weapon!

KNIFE

This blade might look small, but it is sharp enough to open even the toughest, scaliest of Beast-flesh — as we learned when we were face-to-face with Torpix the Twisting Serpent!

FOLDING SPEAR

A recent Avantian innovation, these spears can be folded into three, to make it easier for Questers to carry on long journeys. But don't be fooled — they're deadly when extended!

HARP

Don't mistake this for something pleasant, just because it can be used to make music. Nock an arrow to the harp strings, take aim and fire — you'll see your accuracy greatly improved!

SILVER DISC

This razor-sharp disc was light in my hand, but absolutely deadly when thrown. It was the only thing that could save us from Lustor the Acid Dart!

Now you've seen some of the weapons I've used on my Quests, think about the kind of weapons you'd like to use. Draw them in the space provided, and be sure to make a list of all the magical powers that make them special. Remember — these weapons might have to prove the difference between success and failure on a Quest, so make sure they're useful!

DESIGN YOUR OWN SHIELD

TOM'S MOST VALUABLE TOOL ON HIS BEAST QUESTS IS DEFINITELY HIS SHIELD. EVER SINCE WIZARD ADURO GAVE IT TO HIM, BEFORE HIS VERY FIRST QUEST, IT HAS SAVED TOM'S SKIN MORE TIMES THAN HE CAN COUNT.

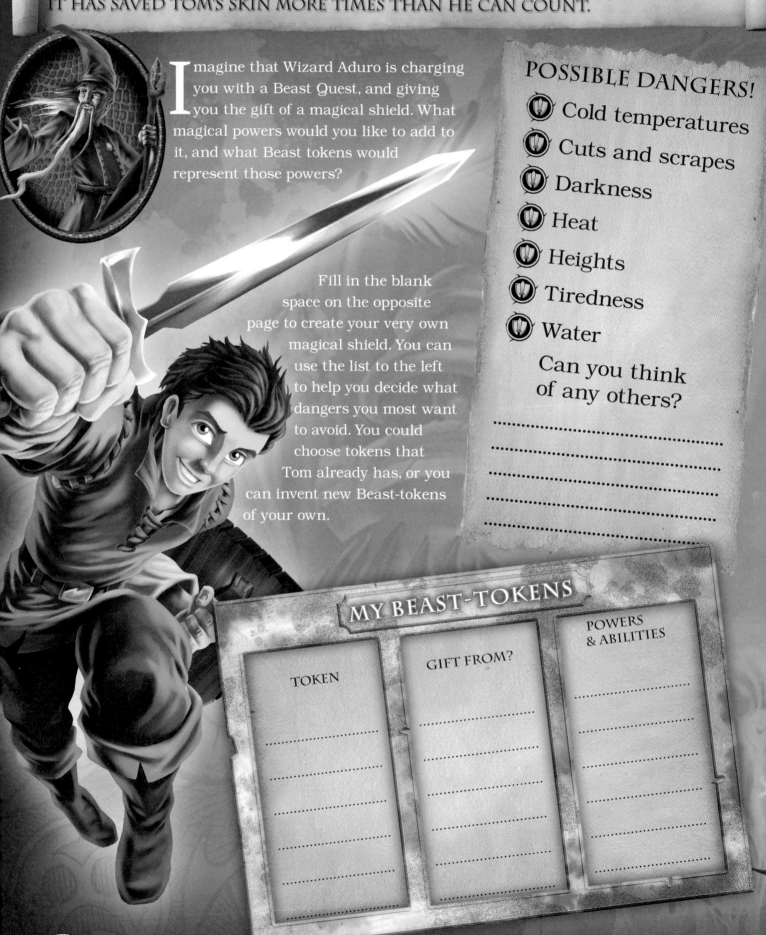

Imagine that Wizard Aduro is charging you with a Beast Quest, and giving you the gift of a magical shield. What magical powers would you like to add to it, and what Beast tokens would represent those powers?

Fill in the blank space on the opposite page to create your very own magical shield. You can use the list to the left to help you decide what dangers you most want to avoid. You could choose tokens that Tom already has, or you can invent new Beast-tokens of your own.

POSSIBLE DANGERS!

- Cold temperatures
- Cuts and scrapes
- Darkness
- Heat
- Heights
- Tiredness
- Water

Can you think of any others?

....
....
....
....

MY BEAST-TOKENS

TOKEN	GIFT FROM?	POWERS & ABILITIES

SHIELD ....'S

Beasts of Kayonia

THE GOLDEN VALLEY

MEATON

THE ICY DESERT

KAYONIAN PLAINS

KAYONIAN FOREST

KAYONIAN MARSHLANDS

KAYONIA

Until the Evil Wizard Velmal dragged me there, I had never even heard of Kayonia. It is not accessible by any path or ocean you'll see on a Gwildorian or Avantian map — dark magic must first rip open a portal, which shimmers with colours that look like a fallen rainbow. Then travellers must steel themselves for the journey — the portal will feel like the fastest, most dangerous chute, which will shunt you in every direction, turning you upside down and spinning you around and around and around...

When you arrive in Kayonia, you will be dizzy and confused from the journey, but you must gather your wits as quickly as you can. They don't nickname this kingdom the "World of Chaos" for nothing! Queen Romaine is an honourable leader, whose intentions are good, but Kayonia has never been the most peaceful of realms. Unrest is constantly stirring, and worsened considerably when Evil comes to visit...

TRAVELLER'S TIPS

1. Try to find your way to Meaton, the capital city in the southeast of Kayonia. You will feel safer in a more crowded area.

2. Stay away from the Golden Valley. There may be great riches in the mines there, but no amount of gold is worth working so close to the terrifying bat-fiend, Fang, whose dark magic can slowly rob you of your sight!

3. After you have left Kayonia, check and double-check that you actually have returned home, as planned. When Tom and Elenna left the ominous kingdom, they found themselves not in Avantia, but in Tavania — a very different place!

Beast Battle!

We must return to Mortaxe's Arena. Maximus is striking again! This time, he has brought Kronus the Clawed Menace for a duel. Study the profile of Kronus, then help me choose the best opponent for this Beast Battle. Remember, since Kronus has wings, this battle will take place in the skies above Mortaxe's Arena — but will a land-Beast confuse the Evil vulture?

STRENGTH

Kronus's oily wings smell absolutely dreadful — if you stand too close to them for too long, you could pass out from the stench! You must try to defeat Kronus as quickly as you can!

STRENGTH

This Beast has red eyes that can shoot beams of light powerful enough to cut through stone and ice — they can also blind you if you look directly at them!

WEAKNESS

The key to defeating any winged-Beast is to get behind it. Its wings and head cannot strike an opponent on its back. If you can take control of the Beast from the rear, victory can be yours!

AGE:	313
POWER:	280
MAGIC LEVEL:	191
FRIGHT FACTOR:	98

KRONUS

EPOS

AGE:	457
POWER:	243
MAGIC LEVEL:	192
FRIGHT FACTOR:	92

STRENGTH

Epos can conjure balls of flame between her talons, making it very difficult for opponents to get close enough to her.

WEAKNESS

But her flame-power is strongest when she is in her lair, the Stonewin Volcano. There's no telling how powerful Epos will be in the Mortaxe's Arena...

WEAKNESS

If Kronus was able to strike out at Arcta's face, and blind the Mountain Giant, my old friend could be in serious danger...

STRENGTH

Against a winged Beast, my instinct is to use another winged Beast, but I wonder... Would Arcta's long legs and arms be able to snatch Kronus from the air, and take this fight to the ground – where wings are useless?

ARCTA

AGE:	324
POWER:	132
MAGIC LEVEL:	120
FRIGHT FACTOR:	65

WEAKNESS

As powerful as she is, Hawkite is occasionally too powerful for her own good. If she's not careful, she can fly too fast, right past her enemies – and crafty Beasts can take advantage of that!

HAWKITE

AGE:	457
POWER:	211
MAGIC LEVEL:	159
FRIGHT FACTOR:	88

STRENGTH

Kronus might be able to cut through stone, but Hawkite's eyes can hypnotise her opponents, and make it impossible for them to move.

All three of these Beasts would give Kronus a good fight, and I know I should fight a winged Beast in the air, but I'm curious as to how Arcta might fare in this scenario... Who do YOU think I should choose?

I think Tom should choose_____

THE CHALLENGER...

One of the most feared Beasts of all is Mortaxe. The Skeleton Warrior was once a loyal friend of Tanner's, but his story took some dark turns after the era of the First Master. With his time having passed, Mortaxe would retreat into deep slumber, for many years at a time. But when he awoke, it would signal that devastation was about to fall upon the kingdom — for, when Mortaxe arose, so too would his Combat Arena. History records a battle that took place approximately two hundred years before Tom set off on his very first Quest — a battle that would change the course of Avantian history.

While he slept, Mortaxe the Skeleton Warrior was not at rest, but neither was he contained. He was not at peace as a reward for his service to Avantia, nor was he being punished for transgressions committed while under the thrall of Evil magic. It was as though Mortaxe's spirit was suspended between life and death.

Each time he awoke, it seemed to him that no time at all had passed since the last time Beasts had been drawn to his Arena to engage in epic, occasionally catastrophic, combat.

But the Beast-combatants came less frequently these days. After centuries of war and civil strife, the kingdom was shaking off the eras of conflict, and embracing a period of balance, peace and order.

But one winter's day, that threatened to change.

As a combatant arrived on the Central Plains with battle in his heart, the ground rumbled and shook. The herd of cattle who had been idly grazing that day scattered in terror, as the earth broke from below, dirt spraying like water. Mortaxe's Combat Arena was returning to Avantia...

Rising with the Arena was Mortaxe himself, who stood up to his full, terrifying height. As he stretched his limbs, the bony cracks and snaps echoing over the Central Plains. He brandished his sharp scythe, whirling it over his head as he cast his gaze around his Arena, wondering which Beast had arrived — and which Beast was to be its opponent.

But there was no Beast to be seen. Only a human, not much more than a boy. He wore gleaming bronze armour, and brandished a most curious weapon — a curved sword on the end of a black whip. Mortaxe stared straight at him, waiting to hear the young man's thoughts, or sense his intentions — but all was silent.

This traveller was no Master of the Beasts. So what was he doing here?

Mortaxe got his answer when he noticed that the man's gaze was fixed not on the Skeleton Warrior's eye-sockets, but on the hole in his sternum — where the bones had been broken, to reveal the heart of the rabid bull-Beast, Krindok, which had been forcibly installed by the Evil Wizard Jaitar.

That's his prize, Mortaxe thought. *He's here to harvest my heart!*

While he was no longer fully under Jaitar's Evil spell, the corrupted heart had long warped Mortaxe so that barely a trace of his former human self — Tarik, friend and soldier-companion of Tanner, the First Master — now remained. When he was made to fight, Mortaxe fought only for himself, and not the kingdom. But if faced with fighting someone he could so easily defeat, Tarik's humanity would swell within the dark heart in his chest, reminding him he should not slaughter an innocent.

He whirled his scythe some more, showing off his skill. When the young man responded by whirling his whip-blade, Mortaxe threw back his head and let his teeth chatter together in an eerie laugh, the sound ricocheting off the walls of the vast, empty arena. His message was clear:

You have no hope.

But the human did not back off. He just twirled his whip-blade over and over. He spoke words, but Mortaxe could not hear them, because this was not a Master armed with a magical token that allowed him to communicate with Beasts. This was just a mercenary, looking to cause mischief, and maybe destruction.

Mortaxe cocked his head in curiosity, baffled as to why this mercenary — armed with only one weapon — would be so bold as to challenge a Beast in his own lair. He got his answer when a thick shadow fell over him.

The young man was not a Challenger... He was distraction!

A huge bird-Beast was swooping over Mortaxe, but this was unlike any he had encountered before. Beneath its black wings was a four-legged body more like a cat's, its claws as cruel and sharp as its curved yellow beak.

This Beast was Vigrash the Clawed Eagle — a ferocious fiend whose favourite trick was to snatch victims from the ground, carry them up into the sky and then drop them from a great height, before gobbling up their smashed bodies like morsels of food.

As Vigrash plummeted down into the Arena, Mortaxe swung his scythe as hard as he could. He missed the Beast, his blade striking the stone floor with a dull clang, and his momentum almost took him off his feet. As the Evil Beast passed over his head, she kicked out her back legs like a horse, sending Mortaxe sprawling forward, right into the path of the human, who whipped his blade, which clattered off Mortaxe's armour, right above the exposed hole in his bony chest.

A few inches lower, and he would have pierced Mortaxe's heart.

The Skeleton Warrior snarled and swatted at the man, who scrambled aside with a yelp of fear — which soon turned to a cry of triumph, for Vigrash had changed course, pouncing on the distracted Mortaxe to clamp his foreclaws on his heavily armoured shoulders.

Vigrash tugged, trying to lift Mortaxe from the ground, but Mortaxe fell to his knees, sinking all his weight down to make sure he was not stolen away from the Arena. He stabbed his scythe into the stone, making it into an anchor, as Vigrash jabbed her eagle head down to peck and nip at him with her beak. Over and over again she struck, making holes in Mortaxe's armour, the curved edges of her beak soon chipping away at Mortaxe's bony shoulders — but he would not yield to the Clawed Eagle.

This Arena was his territory. He was the master here!

With a rattle of rage, Mortaxe took a huge risk. He released the grip on his scythe, which fell with a clatter onto the stony ground, then reached up to take two handfuls of Vigrash's tawny fur. He dragged the Beast off his shoulder and slammed her down onto the ground, again and again, before taking her by the hind-legs and spinning around and around and around.

He tossed Vigrash all the way out of the Arena, and watched with triumph as the Clawed Eagle flapped to right herself, before flying away fast. She had obviously conceded this fight to the Skeleton Warrior!

Mortaxe stamped his boot, sending a tremor through the Arena which knocked his scythe up into his hand — and made the human intruder stagger back with a terrified whimper. Though he couldn't understand what the wretch was saying, Mortaxe could hear a pleading tone in his voice, and it was clear that the young man knew better than to continue his challenge. He dropped his whip-blade, and then scampered out of the Arena.

Mortaxe doubted he would ever see him again. The Central Plains rumbled with a sound like another powerful earthquake once again, as the Combat Arena began to sink, disappearing into the earth from which it had arisen. Only, this time, Mortaxe was not sinking with it.

His destination was somewhere else...

For having repelled an Evil Beast from Avantia, Mortaxe had earned a redemption that trumped the Dark Heart that had been foisted upon him by Jaitar. From that day on, he would lie beneath the Palace, in the Gallery of Tombs, side-by-side with Tanner. He would lie there for over two centuries, until a new villain would resurrect him...

DRAGONS!

THE FIRST BEAST TOM AND I EVER FACED TOGETHER WAS A DRAGON, AND WE HAVE BATTLED MANY MORE SINCE THEN. YOU'D THINK WE'D BE 'USED TO' DRAGONS BY NOW, BUT GIANT, SCALY, FIRE-BREATHING CREATURES ARE NOT EASY TO 'GET USED TO'. IN FACT, THEY ARE NEVER LESS THAN ABSOLUTELY DEADLY!

STRENGTH

Ferno's fire can scorch even metal, while his thick dragon scales protect him from even the sharpest of blades.

FERNO

AGE:	288
POWER:	212
MAGIC LEVEL:	180
FEAR FACTOR:	91

WEAKNESS

Ferno is vulnerable to attacks from his back — but few get close enough to take him unawares!

STRENGTH

These Beasts are only discovering the full extent of their powers, which makes them more energetic than the average Beast. Their youth also makes them fearless...

VEDRA AND KRIMON

	VEDRA	KRIMON
AGE:	1	1
POWER:	150	131
MAGIC LEVEL:	126	146
FEAR FACTOR:	50	50

WEAKNESS

...but fearless Beasts can be restless Beasts. Their exuberance can sometimes get them into trouble!

BLAZE

AGE:	313
POWER:	210
MAGIC LEVEL:	187
FEAR FACTOR:	90

STRENGTH

Unlike most dragons, Blaze does not breathe fire, but ice — which can turn any attacker into a frozen statue!

WEAKNESS

Blaze is fearsome, but his body is more slender than most Beasts. A strong opponent might be able to pin him down.

STRENGTH

We've seen that some dragons breathe fire, and others breathe ice, but Torno's specialty is using his vast wings to create powerful winds that keep his enemy at a distance. His long arms and claws also make him dangerous at close-quarters.

TORNO

AGE:	256
POWER:	267
MAGIC LEVEL:	181
FEAR FACTOR:	91

WEAKNESS

His wings can create fierce gusts, but they are also the weakest part of his body — strong swipes of a sword, or fierce Beast-punches, can do some serious damage, and restrict his ability to fly!

DODGING A DRAGON

I would strongly recommend you steer clear of a dragon if ever you come across one — I only take the risk because my shield can protect me from fire and ice. But if you ever do have to get close to a dragon, be very careful — fire and smoke are deadly. A good survival technique is to breathe through a wet rag or towel, held close to your face. If you can remember, bite down on the towel when you apply it — this will stop you breathing through your mouth!

DRAGONS HATCH FROM EGGS THAT LIE IN CAVES FOR HUNDREDS OF YEARS UNTIL THE BEAST IS READY TO BE BORN. FOLLOW THIS RECIPE TO MAKE YOUR OWN DRAGON EGGS - BUT BE CAREFUL WHERE YOU LEAVE THEM! PRECIOUS EGGS LIKE THESE ARE TARGETS FOR NEFARIOUS THIEVES!

DRAGON EGGS

WHAT YOU NEED TO MAKE DRAGON EGGS

- Eggs
- Water
- Saucepan
- Stove
- Food colouring
- Containers - cups or glasses (big enough for eggs!)
- Fork/spoon

1. ASK AN ADULT to boil water in the saucepan, on the stove. When the water is boiling, ask them to place the eggs inside. Set a timer for between 7-10 minutes, and wait...

2. Once the eggs are boiled, ASK AN ADULT to take them out. Allow them to cool down for a few minutes. Once they are cool, use a fork or a spoon to make cracks in the shell – as if a Baby Dragon is about to be born!

3. Pour food colouring into the cup or glass, then place the egg inside. (Be Careful not to get any on your hands – wash them immediately afterwards!)

4. Allow the eggs to sit in the dye for at least an hour – but closer to three hours will create better results.

5. Take the eggs out of the dye, and use kitchen roll to dry them off.

Beast Quests can occasionally involve a lot of waiting around. True heroes know the value of patience!

6. Now, slowly peel away the shell to reveal the Beastly design underneath!

DRAGON SKIN CHEST

ON THEIR BEAST QUESTS, TOM AND ELENNA USUALLY HAVE LOTS OF IMPORTANT ITEMS THEY HAVE TO CARRY, WHICH MIGHT BE TOO FRAGILE TO STASH IN STORM☐S SADDLEBAG... AND TOO VALUABLE TO STORE IN ANY MAKESHIFT DEN THEY HAVE TO LEAVE BEHIND TO BATTLE A BEAST. SOMETHING NEEDS TO BE DONE! ONE IDEA WOULD BE TO HELP THEM MAKE A SMALL CHEST THAT LOOKS TOO SCARY FOR ANY PASSING THIEVES TO STEAL. HOW TO DO THAT? MAKE IT SO THAT THE CHEST LOOKS LIKE IT IS MADE OF DRAGON SKIN!

1. With the help of an adult, photocopy — or scan and print — the lid, base and divider templates on Pages 75, 76 and 77.

2. Use the glue to stick each template on the card, and then CAREFULLY use the scissors to cut them out, using the dotted lines as guides.

3. Fold each section along the lines indicated.

4. Glue the lid together, using the tabs as indicated. Press firmly, to make sure it is shut correctly, and then leave to dry.

5. While the lid is drying, glue the base together, using the tabs as indicated. Press firmly, to make sure it is shut correctly, and then leave to dry.

6. While the lid and the base are drying, CAREFULLY use the scissors to cut the slots in the divider pieces as indicated. Now, slot them together. Put the completed divider in the base of the Chest. Now, you have made compartments for all of Tom and Elenna's valuables!

7. Once all the glue has dried, place the lid on top of the base, as indicated. Your chest is almost complete. Now, for the finishing touches…

8. Use the paints to make the paper look like dragon skin — make it as scary as possible. Tom can't afford to lose ANY of his precious tokens!

FOR THIS, YOU WILL NEED:

- A helpful, watchful adult
- Access to a photocopier, or a scanner and printer
- Card, preferably strong and sturdy
- Scissors — BE CAREFUL
- Glue — WASH YOUR HANDS AFTERWARDS
- Assorted paints — preferably greens, yellows and purples

glue glue glue glue

glue Lid to base

glue glue glue glue

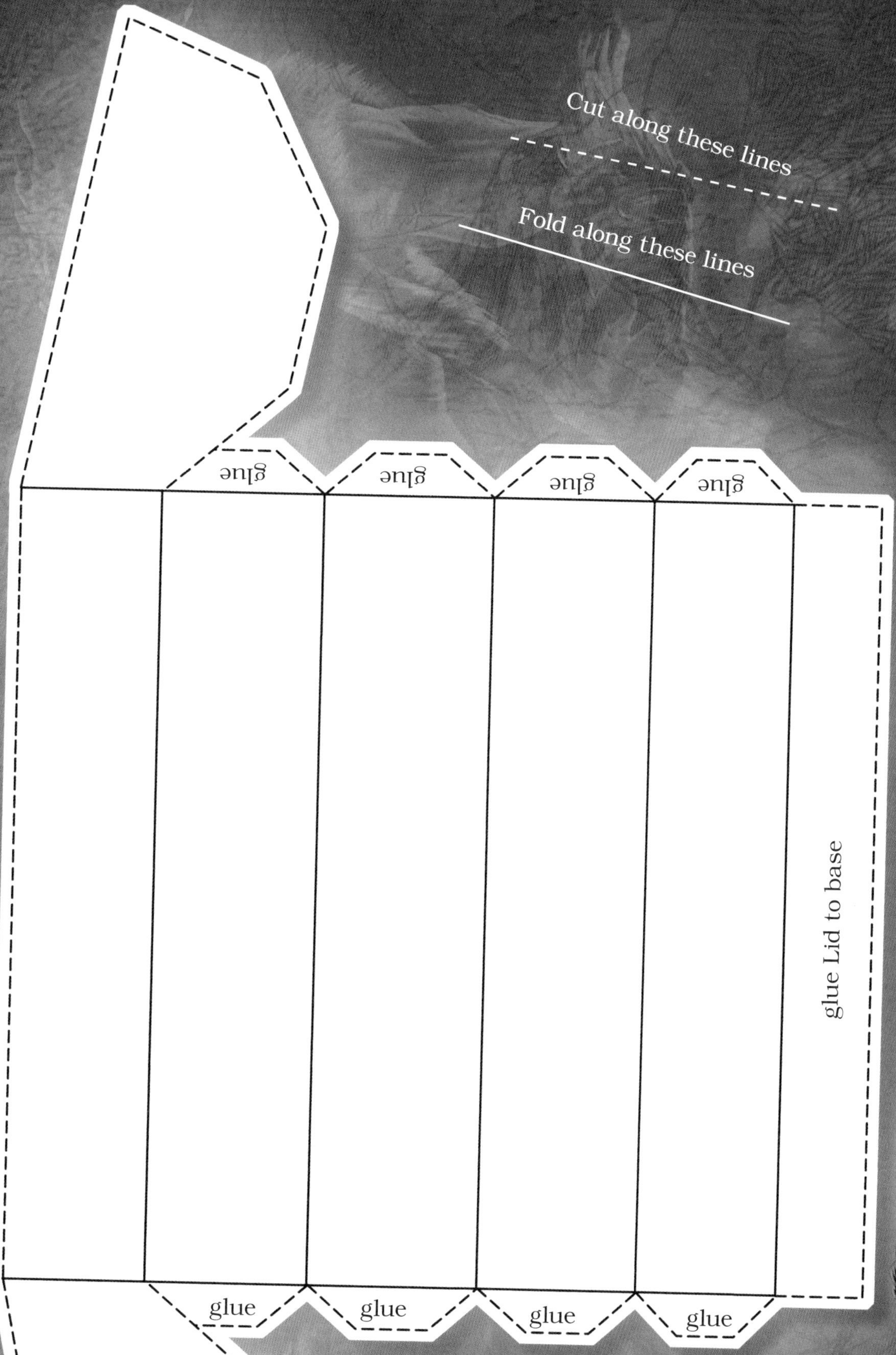

YOU COULD DRAW SCALES LIKE
THESE ON YOUR BOX!

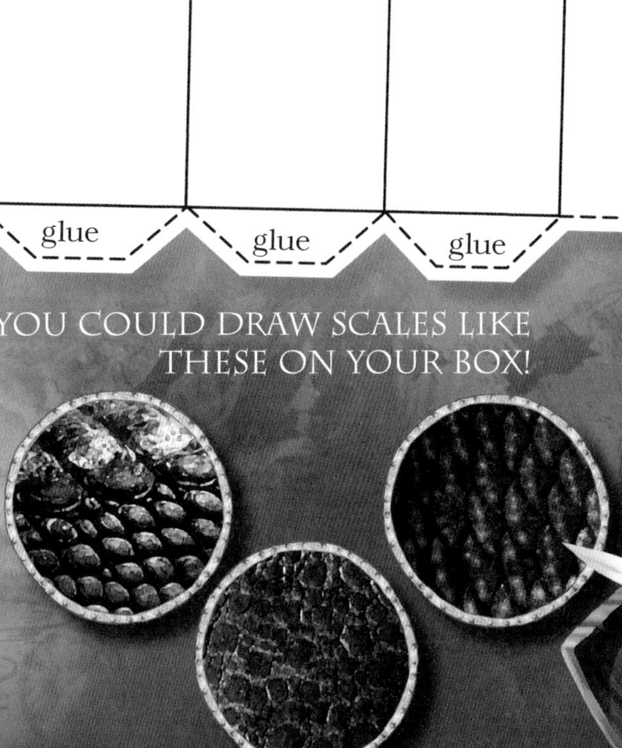

Cut along these lines

Fold along these lines

glue

glue

glue

glue

76

Beast Battle!

Another battle is about to break out in Mortaxe's Arena. Maximus has cast a spell on Hellion, and turned him into a Beast of destruction. I must choose a champion to subdue the Fiery Foe, but which Beast is the best suited to tackle such a fearsome opponent?

STRENGTH

Hellion is as tall as a house, and his body is made of flame. The slightest touch can set you on fire in seconds — and if you let the Beast curl into a ball, he will roll on the ground at speed, torching everything he touches.

STRENGTH

Because of the heat given off by the flames, Hellion's limbs can keep most opponents at an even greater distance — even if you avoid being burned, the heat up close is unbearable!

WEAKNESS

Fire is frightening, but if you can extinguish the flames somehow, Hellion will shrink, and his powers will disappear.

AGE: 297

POWER: 235

MAGIC LEVEL: 159

FRIGHT FACTOR: 82

HELLION

DOOMSKULL

AGE:	339
POWER:	222
MAGIC LEVEL:	141
FRIGHT FACTOR:	83

STRENGTH

Doomskull's muscular body is made of rippling stone muscles. It will be very hard for Hellion to set him on fire!

WEAKNESS

As powerful as he is, Doomskull has a four-legged form that makes him vulnerable to attack from more flexible opponents. If Hellion can take his back and hold him down, Doomskull will be in trouble!

WEAKNESS

Grashkor's helmet might guard against serious injury, but it also limits his eyesight. If Hellion's flame attacks from the side, he might not see the danger until it's too late...

GRASHKOR

AGE:	257
POWER:	289
MAGIC LEVEL:	150
FRIGHT FACTOR:	80

STRENGTH

Grashkor might be well-suited to battling Hellion because of his armour, which can protect him from flame; also, his long whip might be able to do damage from a safe distance.

WEAKNESS

If the Arctic Warrior doesn't finish this fight quickly, his body could start melting from his opponent's heat — and that would be a disaster!

KOLDO

AGE:	335
POWER:	183
MAGIC LEVEL:	166
FRIGHT FACTOR:	84

STRENGTH

Against a fiery Beast, maybe cold ice could work to counter the flame? Koldo's club-limb might do damage to Hellion, and help to douse the flame, exposing his weaker body beneath?

Fire is so dangerous, I'm tempted to pick Grashkor, because of his armour and whip. I really don't want Koldo to melt, and I'm not sure I trust Doomskull, even though I know he could be a tough opponent for Hellion.

What do YOU think?

I think Tom should choose_____

Henkrall

FORESTED STARMOUND

GREAT NORTHERNET NORTHMARKET

GREED ISLAND

THE PLAINS

DESERT

VELORA

SENSA'S CASTLE

THE SEA-CLIFF

HENKRALL

Most visitors to Henkrall are intimidated by the sight of the Sea-Cliff in the west, and for good reason — one slip, and you are falling fast, right to your doom. But the people of Henkrall tend not to worry about falls, even from such great heights. Why? Because the people there — Henkrallians? I think that might be what they're called, but I don't actually care! — have wings. This makes them almost impossible to catch — which is why I chopped off Igor's wings when I made him my slave!

Even the animals have wings in Henkrall! Because of this, people from a town on one side of the kingdom can travel very fast to places all the way on the other side, which makes for a frustratingly peaceful community!

Do I regret leaving Henkrall behind? Some days, I do — I had my own castle there, and I was the only Sorceress, which meant that the Henkrallians, or whatever they're called (I still don't care!), feared me. I liked that. But then again… it was time to return to Avantia, the kingdom that exiled me — and to Sanpao, my partner-in-crime — so that I could claim it for myself!

TRAVELLER'S TIPS

1. If you don't have wings, watch where you step — there's always a good chance your next one will take you off a cliff.

2. If a kind winged person from Henkrall offers you a lift, it is good manners to hold on to their shoulders, NEVER their wings! Feathers are sensitive!

BEASTS OF THE MOUNTAINS

BEAST QUESTS THAT TAKE US TO MOUNTAINS ARE A SPECIAL CHALLENGE - NOT ONLY ARE WE FACING UP TO ANOTHER FEROCIOUS MONSTER, BUT WE ALSO HAVE TO DEAL WITH VERTIGO! THE MOUNTAINS DEMAND ALL OF OUR COURAGE, AND FOCUS – WORRYING ABOUT THE HEIGHT IS A DISTRACTION THAT CAN MEAN OUR QUEST WILL END WITH A TERRIBLE FALL!

ARCTA

AGE:	324
POWER:	132
MAGIC LEVEL:	120
FEAR FACTOR:	65

WEAKNESS

Arcta's size has a dual disadvantage – he can be clumsy. A Beast with great speed and swiftness might be able to exploit this!

STRENGTH

One of the earliest Beasts we faced, and Arcta remains one of the largest. He is strong enough to rip chunks of rock from the mountains and throw them great distances! If you're nearby when he does this, take cover!

RASHOUK

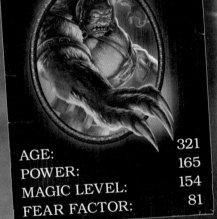

AGE:	321
POWER:	165
MAGIC LEVEL:	154
FEAR FACTOR:	81

WEAKNESS

The best way to defeat a Cave Troll is to lure him out of his cave. His eyes are very sensitive to sunlight and lightning – flashes of light will make him panic, and THEN you can attack!

STRENGTH

The long, yellow nails on Rashouk's left hand will turn you to stone if he manages to scratch you! And good luck trying to strike him – when attackers get too close, Rashouk is able to turn himself into a ghost to avoid attacks!

ROKK

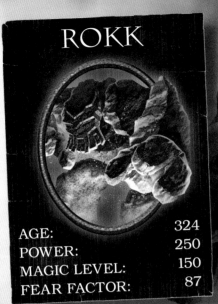

AGE: 324
POWER: 250
MAGIC LEVEL: 150
FEAR FACTOR: 87

STRENGTH

Rokk may be gigantic, but he can still hide in plain sight by camouflaging his rocky body among the mountains. You could be standing in the palm of his hand, and not even know it — until it's too late!

WEAKNESS

Rokk might be vast, but he is made up entirely of rocks and boulders — which are very heavy, making him among the slowest of Beasts. If an attacker keeps his distance, he can easily avoid being crushed...

STRENGTH

The Winged Assassin can bite through flesh with her needle-sharp teeth. The scales of her muscular legs can repel even the sharpest of blades. She is crafty too, distracting victims with her deadly spear before using her huge talons to snatch them right off the ground!

WEAKNESS

Her wings are the weak spot on her body — if you can compromise how well she flies, you might create an opening for a counter attack!

KORAKA

AGE: 25
POWER: 260
MAGIC LEVEL: 167
FEAR FACTOR: 93

HOW TO SURVIVE A MOUNTAIN

Before you even reach the Beasts, there are many difficulties you will face on a Mountain Quest. Climbing high is exhausting, so make sure you only do so at full-strength! It's also good to have a mental check-list of non-Beastly dangers that you should be aware of. For example:

- **Avalanches** — can you hear odd rumbling-noises? Can you feel tremors beneath your feet? They might be warnings of dangerous rockfalls!

- **Cracks in the rock** — if a mountain path has lots of cracks, it might be weak, which means you should probably look for another route.

- **Oxygen** — the air gets thinner at altitude, which makes it harder to breathe, and can cause sickness. Heavier breathing can cause dehydration, so try not to do any serious climbing if you don't have enough water!

A HERO'S PARENTS
TALADON & FREYA

I spent most of my childhood wondering about my father, Taladon, and why he had disappeared when I was just an infant. It was only when I followed in his footsteps, and began protecting the kingdom, that I would learn the truth. But discovering my father was still alive was not the biggest surprise in store for me — I would also learn that I had a mother, who protected a kingdom on the other side of the Western Ocean…

Tom's mother met his father not long after she first became Gwildor's Mistress of the Beasts. Since the two kingdoms shared an ocean, their great water Beasts, Sepron and Krabb, would occasionally encroach on each other's territory. Though they were both Good Beasts, neither would back down, and occasionally the force of their fights would send ripples running through the water, all the way back to the shores of the kingdoms. Believing that Avantia's Sea Serpent was under attack, King Hugo sent his Master of the Beasts, Taladon, to the shore to investigate. Summoning Ferno, Taladon flew out over the Western Ocean, using the enhanced eyesight from his golden helmet to watch for any sign that Sepron was in danger beneath the surface. But it wasn't the surface he needed to worry about — it was the sky…

FREYA

AGE:	44
POWER:	190
MAGIC LEVEL:	170
FEAR FACTOR:	78

At the same moment that Taladon was given his mission to protect Sepron, so too was Gwildor's Mistress of the Beasts given a mission to protect Krabb. Freya was flying Hawkite right at him! The air rattled with the clang of their swords, as Mistress and Master duelled in the sky, neither one knowing that they were, in fact, both on the side of Good. Ferno breathed fire, but Hawkite beat his wings, creating a gust powerful enough to send the flames back at the dragon — and Taladon, who was knocked off the Beast's back and plunged into the sea!

Unable to bear letting another person drown — even one she believed to be Evil — Freya guided Hawkite to fly low, so that she could rescue her opponent. Seeing her save his Master's life convinced Ferno not to continue his attack; and now that things were calm, Taladon could explain who he was and why he was here. Realising they both had the same goal — peace in the ocean — the Master and Mistress worked together to calm the tensions between Krabb and Sepron, establishing a formidable partnership that would bring the kingdom of Avantia and the kingdom of Gwildor closer together than ever before...

TALADON

AGE: 48
POWER: 201
MAGIC LEVEL: 176
FEAR FACTOR: 80

A BEASTLY GIFT!

The first Master of the Beasts was a warrior called Tanner. Elenna and I have read about some of his earliest exploits protecting the kingdom in the fabled "Chronicles of Avantia," but he undertook many Quests and adventures in his lifetime. This is one of mine and Elenna's favourites…

Slow down," Castor called. "My horse is getting tired!"

Ever since Tanner had tamed the grey stallion they had encountered roaming the Central Plains — the stallion he had named Thunder — Castor had struggled to keep up. His own white mare, Star, was no slouch, but Thunder seemed to never tire, no matter how hard Tanner pushed him.

Today, Tanner was pushing him very hard. "We can't slow down," he said. "Firepos is in danger."

Since their defeat of the evil warlord, Derthsin, Tanner had felt a deeper connection with the Flame-Bird. And today, even from his village of Forton, a days' ride south of Firepos's home, the Stonewin Volcano, he had the nagging worry that his lifelong Beast friend was in danger.

It had been over a year since Anoret, the First Beast, had dropped Derthsin into the volcano, bringing relative peace to the land. Although there was still the odd cluster of leftover mercenaries, they kept their mischief to small villages, and always fled when one of Avantia's heroes showed up to fight them. Surely they wouldn't be stupid enough to challenge a phoenix in her volcano home?

Tanner knew this was true, but he also knew that he ought to listen to his gut… and his gut was telling him Firepos was in trouble.

And when he and Castor came within sight of the Stonewin Volcano, his gut plummeted when he saw that he had been right to be afraid.

A pack of varkules were clambering up the stony slopes.

The two boys slowed their horses to a stop. "Every time we run these things off, I hope it's the last we see of them," Castor growled. "But it never is!" He sighed, leaning forward to stroke Star's mane. "I need you to run some more, girl," he said. "But I promise, once this is all over, I will bring you all the carrots you can eat!"

The two boys dug their heels into their horses' sides, spurring them on to gallop forward and up the slope of the volcano. The clip-clop of their hooves on the stone alerted the varkules, who growled furiously as they turned, moving as one. Tanner and Castor drew their swords from their hips. Both boys swiped their weapons, keeping the vicious varkules from getting too close to their horses.

The sun over Stonewin bounced off their flashing blades as the heroes hacked and slashed at the varkules, who pounced forward and snapped their slavering jaws. One got so close that Castor's blade sliced off the sharp points of its lower fangs, sending the creature scurrying away, squealing in pain. But Tanner had found himself dealing with a pair of varkules launching a twin-attack.

"Arrrgghhh!" Tanner cried out as a varkule's jaws clamped down on his sword-arm, just above the wrist. The animal gave a tug with its head and dragged both Tanner and Thunder down to the stony ground. Tanner released the reins so that Thunder could scramble clear, and let go of his sword so that he could snatch it up with his free hand. But the varkule was not letting go…

…and Castor could not reach him, because his way was barred by a trio of varkules.

At that moment, a deep growl rumbled through the Stonewin Volcano, so powerful that Tanner feared it was about to erupt. When the top of the structure broke off, sending a storm of rock raining down on all of them, he was convinced of it. In terror, the attacking varkule released its grip on Tanner's arm and joined its pack in scampering away, as the mighty form of Firepos loomed overhead, her wingspan so vast she blocked out the sun and threw a cloak of darkness over them.

The varkules soon disappeared in the distance, as Firepos lowered herself to the ground. She folded her flame-tipped wings and gazed down at Tanner, her ruby eyes glimmering with concern. Tanner noticed she was looking at his arm, from which blood still gushed where the varkule had bitten him.

"You should tear off a sleeve," said Castor, who was dismounting from Star. "That will stop the—" He yelped when Firepos extended her legs, wrapping one of her claws around Tanner's wounded arm.

Tanner tried to back away, but the Beast held him fast. What was happening? Had Firepos somehow turned to evil?

But she just helped us fight the varkules…

Only when a warm feeling passed through Tanner's arm, replacing the throbbing ache where the varkule had bitten him, did he understand. Firepos was healing his wound.

After Tanner's arm was restored to health, the Flame-Bird took to the air again, and with a flap of her wings, floated up back towards the volcano.

"Look, Tanner," said Castor, pointing at the ground. Tanner gazed down and saw that, among a small cluster of stones and broken rocks, a curious object lay waiting for him. It was a gift from Firepos… A phoenix talon!

From that day forward, every Master of the Beasts in Avantia was gifted Epos's phoenix talon, one of the most precious and valuable tokens to have with you on a Beast Quest!

LOST BEASTS!

KENSA AND SANPAO ARE UP TO THEIR TRICKS AGAIN – THEY'VE STOLEN BEASTS AND HIDDEN THEM AWAY! YOU MUST HELP TOM FIND THEM ALL. EACH BEAST NAME COULD BE UP, DOWN, LEFT, RIGHT OR DIAGONAL. SOME NAMES WILL SHARE THE SAME LETTERS, AND SOME HAVE BEEN FLIPPED BACKWARDS!

CAN YOU FIND:

ARAX
ARCTA
BRUTUS
CLAW
EPOS
FANG
FERNO
GRASHKOR
KAYMON
KILDOR
KOLDO
KRABB
KRAGOS
KRIMON
NANOOK
RAVIRA
ROKK
SEPRON
SKOR
SLIVKA
STING
TAGUS
TARGRO
TUSK
VEDRA
ZEPHA

S	Q	K	A	Y	M	O	N	T	Y	Y	X	A	R	A
A	K	O	O	N	A	N	K	E	X	O	V	N	S	T
G	R	T	G	Y	K	J	O	A	C	H	D	W	G	C
T	A	G	Y	O	V	F	N	L	S	D	W	L	P	R
E	B	R	A	V	I	R	A	G	H	A	C	L	O	A
Y	B	A	E	E	L	W	A	N	I	E	Q	S	Q	K
U	M	S	G	D	S	A	W	E	G	P	H	L	S	O
I	E	H	I	R	I	E	A	F	A	O	D	U	F	O
O	Y	K	A	A	F	W	P	E	A	S	T	I	N	G
S	K	O	R	K	B	O	O	R	O	K	K	O	G	O
A	I	R	X	I	K	R	I	N	O	G	O	F	H	R
H	L	P	A	I	M	G	U	O	V	N	K	E	I	G
P	D	A	N	G	P	O	H	T	X	P	E	D	S	R
E	O	X	F	G	O	S	N	L	U	W	H	A	V	A
Z	R	T	E	E	I	S	A	Q	U	S	U	G	A	T

SHADE IN EACH WORD AS YOU FIND IT. THE LETTERS IN THE RED BOXES WILL REVEAL THE NAME OF TWO SPECIAL BEASTS TOM NEEDS TO HELP HIM ON THIS QUEST!

ESCAPE THE MAZE!

Disaster! The Ghost Beasts have escaped the Forbidden Land, and have cornered Elenna in a terrifying maze. It's so dark in there that she can't see very well — a Beast could be around any corner.

You must guide her safely out of the maze to where Tom is waiting for her — but be careful to avoid the Ghost Beasts. One wrong turn, and Elenna will be walking right into her doom!

89

Beasts of Seraph

REDWELL

THE EASTERN FOREST

THE ETERNAL FLAME

THE SNOWY NORTH

FISHING VILLAGE

THE RAGING RIVER

THE SEA OF SERAPH

SERAPH

Seraph is a mysterious land. Its borders are narrow, with seas on both sides. One of the more amazing sights is The Raging River — a long, twisty stream that snakes away from the mountain peaks in the central region of the kingdom, all the way to the Sea of Seraph in the west. This river does not end in an estuary, however...

The river becomes a waterfall that, if you're not careful, can drag you to a watery demise!

Of course, there's really only one thing that makes the journey to Seraph worthwhile, and that is the Eternal Flame. About the only thing anyone knows for sure is that it is guarded by the terrifying Beast, Torpix. Even the experts disagree on what powers the Eternal Flame can grant any Quester who finds it. My former mentor, Malvel, sought to burn the Warlock's Staff in this magical fire, hoping that it would endow him with the ultimate power. After Tom drove Malvel into the flame, we thought we'd seen the end of him — but he returned, stronger than ever. So maybe, the myths about the Eternal Flame are absolutely true. I wonder...

STRANGEST BEASTS!

WHEN I WAS GROWING UP, THE WORD 'BEAST' MADE ME THINK OF DRAGONS AND SEA SERPENTS, GIANT LIZARDS AND WINGED MENACES. IN OTHER WORDS, IT MADE ME THINK OF MONSTERS. BUT OCCASIONALLY, TOM AND I ENCOUNTER CREATURES THAT ARE NOT JUST ORDINARY BEASTS, BUT HORRIBLE HYBRIDS OF HUMAN AND MONSTER!

STING

AGE:	15
POWER:	248
MAGIC LEVEL:	162
FEAR FACTOR:	71

WEAKNESS

Sting is not just angry he was turned into a Beast — he is also sad about it, too. This sadness sometimes dampens his will to fight, and leaves him vulnerable to attack.

STRENGTH

Sting can scuttle very fast, and his poisonous tail can paralyse opponents. One of the few Beasts who was originally a human, he is filled with a rage that makes him an even deadlier opponent.

HECTON

AGE:	302
POWER:	294
MAGIC LEVEL:	188
FEAR FACTOR:	96

WEAKNESS

As frightening as he is, Hecton is among the smallest of Beasts, who wields his weapons like a human. A skilled warrior has a chance of surviving a dual against the Body Snatcher — so make sure you practice as often as you can!

STRENGTH

This hideous Beast wears a cloak made of creatures he has killed, with a hollowed-out bull's head for a grisly hood. Most who face him struggle to hold onto their nerve — which leaves them vulnerable to attack from his deadly trident. And even if you avoid this weapon, the green mist Hecton breathes can invade your body, and absorb you into his cloak!

RAKSHA

AGE:	257
POWER:	292
MAGIC LEVEL:	200
FEAR FACTOR:	98

STRENGTH

This armoured demon is able to absorb Tom's shield into his chest, which gives him the signature strengths of Avantia's Good Beasts, which he can use to deadly effect in battle against his opponents.

WEAKNESS

Raksha is not unbeatable, but the way to best him is VERY difficult. You need to use the jewelled Mirror of Raksha to reflect moonlight on the Lake of Light — this will create a spiralling eddy in the water, which can suck the hybrid Beast down!

GRASHKOR

AGE:	257
POWER:	289
MAGIC LEVEL:	150
FEAR FACTOR:	80

STRENGTH

This muscular Beast is equally comfortable fighting on the ground or in the air. His long whip is made up of nine putrid animal bones which ends in a Bull's Skull, with curved horns that can lacerate even the sturdiest of flesh!

WEAKNESS

Like most winged Beasts, Grashkor does not fare well on water — if you can lure him out to sea, and trick him into making a plunge, you can weaken him enough so that he's more vulnerable to sword-attacks!

FUTURE OF STING

Most Beasts we encounter are either friends or enemies — one of the few who is "in between" is Sting. He began as Seth, a young boy who was manipulated by Malvel into becoming his loyal follower, and eventually punished by being transformed into the Scorpion-Man. Elenna and I defeated Sting in battle, but we did not banish him from Gorgonia altogether, and returned to Avantia knowing that he was still out there… somewhere. Deep down in my heart, I know that Sting's story is not over, and that there is another chapter still to be told… I just hope that the next chapter has a happier ending.

A FATEFUL CHOICE

The history of Wizardry in Avantia is littered with heroes and villains, with good deeds and moments of treachery — and pivotal moments where the fate of the kingdom seems to rest on a single decision. A Wizard is likely to face many such decisions in his life, and my Master Aduro always told me that there was one decision he wishes he never made...

Aduro?" King Theo's voice echoed in the palace stables, startling me — worse, it startled the horse I had been hastily saddling, and I had to grip the reins with all my strength to keep it under control. I had been so distracted I had not heard His Majesty's approach. I would have been embarrassed at being taken by surprise, had I not been so preoccupied with the curious vision I had just seen in my crystal ball.

"Magic stirs in the East, Your Majesty," I explained. "Wayward magic, wielded by a boy who is frightened by his own capabilities."

The king smoothed his beard, which hung past his sternum, and adjusted the long, red cloak that flowed from his shoulders.

"Dark magic?" he asked, his face creasing in concern.

"That I don't know," I replied. "But I must get to the East and intervene, before the errant boy can do harm."

His Majesty stepped into the stables, a mild grin on his face and twinkle of amusement in his eyes. "Wouldn't it be easier to transport yourself there via magic? Your riding skills are famously terrible."

Normally, I would join in with the joke. Most Wizards, in most kingdoms, are known to be terrible horsemen — armed with magic that can send us anywhere we want in a puff of smoke, we never need to practice our riding, and so we are hopeless in the saddle. But I could not laugh with the king today, because I was too tense, too unnerved. There had been no indication that a new Sorcerer was to come into being at this time, and it was very worrying that one appeared to have done so.

I told the king. "I know nothing of the boy in the East, but I can tell that he is frightened and unpredictable. His own powers do not just fascinate him — they horrify him, as well. If I was to show up in a puff of smoke, it might push him over the edge."

King Theo nodded. "A wise strategy," he said. "But that does not change the fact you will take more than a day to reach your destination."

"There is no other way, Your Majesty."

That grin again. It seemed to glow through his beard. "Yes, there is."

So King Theo rode me to the East himself. It saved me a lot of time — thankfully, we rode under the cover of night, so there were no subjects to witness the peculiar spectacle of Avantia's ruler leaning forward in the saddle, urging his grey mare to run "quicker, quicker!"

As we rode, I closed my eyes and focused my senses, trying to locate the source of the fear and confusion I could feel emanating from the region. As dawn broke over Avantia, I guided King Hugo all the way to a village just south of Rokwin. To the North, the Stonewin Volcano loomed in the distance, while further East, the barren plains of the Forbidden Land spilled listlessly into the fog that hung over that region — fog so heavy and dense, it seemed to be warning travellers that they ought to turn back.

"Go right," I told the king, who guided the horse along a dirt-road that led to a town so barren it had to have been abandoned years ago. "Are you sure?" the king asked me, as he tugged on the reins to bring the horse to a stop. All around us were rickety huts made of rotting wood. "Most of the communities in the East sought new homes long ago."

I nodded. This was true. Nobody wanted to live so close to the Forbidden Land. But I could sense it — magic, and the frightened boy, was close by.

"Stay here," I told the king, as I slipped down from the saddle.

"You can't go in alone," he protested.

I shook my head at him. "If the boy — whoever he is — sees the king here, he might fear that he is to be arrested. There's no telling what he will do then."

I could tell His Majesty wasn't happy about it, but he nodded anyway. "Very well," he said. "Be careful, Aduro. Avantia needs its Good Wizard."

I smiled at him, trying to look more confident than I felt. I was still relatively young — only twenty-seven years old — and had not yet reached my own full potential. Because of this, I knew I was vulnerable while facing down wayward magic.

But I did not tell King Theo this. I just turned around, and walked into the barren town.

My instincts pulled me towards a ramshackle dwelling, which stood next to a well that had probably run dry many years before. Without being able to see inside, I could sense that magic was behind the wooden walls, which were so rickety I was hesitant to open the door for fear of pulling the whole house down.

As I reached the dwelling, I clenched my fists, ready for anything. In one fluid motion, I pulled open the door and used it as a shield, just in case the errant Wizard behind it sought to attack an intruder.

But there were no bolts of deadly magic aimed wildly in my direction. There was only the sound of whimpering — and a rushing drone that was horribly familiar. I dared to peer around the door, and saw a young boy in tatty green robes huddled in one corner, near the door, staring amazed at the swirling sphere of purple light that completely covered the far wall.

"I didn't mean to," the boy wailed, when he saw me. "I don't know how this happened…"

"It's all right," I told him, stepping into the house and extending a hand. "I know you didn't mean to do anything wrong." I was sounding confident, but inside I was frightened. Wherever that portal led, I knew it wasn't likely to be anywhere good. I had to close it as soon as possible — but first, I had to get this frightened boy away from it. "What's your name?" I asked him.

"M-M-M…" he stuttered. "Malvel!"

"Listen to me, Malvel," I said. "I need you to take my hand. Then I need you to stand up and walk out of here, while I deal with the portal. Do you think you can do that? "Malvel did not get to answer — because, at that moment, a Beast came striding through the portal…

I did not hesitate. I sprang to my feet, stood upright and aimed two bolts of magical light at the Beast stepping through the portal. I knew this creature to be Torgor, the Minotaur from Gorgonia. He hefted his terrifying gold axe to deflect my magic, the ricochets tearing holes in the wooden ceiling.

"Run!" I shouted to Malvel, as the house started to fall in on itself. I stooped to take two handfuls of the boy's tatty robes, and dragged him clear just as the house collapsed on top of Torgor.

Outside, Malvel surveyed the wreckage. "Is it… dead?" he asked, his voice hoarse and wheezy with fear and exertion. King Theo had galloped up to us both on the grey horse, his face a mask of concern.

"Are you hurt?" he asked. I shook my head. "We should get out of here, though," I said. "That mountain of debris won't contain Torgor for very long."

Barely were the words out of my mouth, than the collapsed house seemed to erupt, as Torgor used his axe to scatter the clumps of wood in all directions.

Once he was free, he charged at us again.

"Stand back!" the king hollered, drawing his sword and running to intercept the Beast. His Majesty fought bravely, without fear, ducking swipes of Torgor's axe and landing blows of his own. But no ordinary blade could wound a minotaur, not with the thick, coarse pelt which protected his flesh as well as any armour. Soon, the king tired, and his strikes became listless and lazy.

Torgor swatted him aside and sent the king crashing into another one of the rickety houses, which buckled and collapsed on top of him.

Beside me, young Malvel clutched at my robes in utter terror.

"What do we do now!?"

I closed my eyes and concentrated, sending out a message across the kingdom.

Beasts of Avantia… Your kingdom needs you!

Given that we were in the East, I expected the Flame-Bird Epos to be the first to answer the call, but I was wrong. In the distance behind me, the sound of hooves pounding the dirt-road was carried by the wind.

Tagus was here!

The Horse-Man's territory was the Central Plains, which was a long way from this desolate town in the shadow of Stonewin. Quite what he was doing patrolling far away from it, I didn't know — all that mattered was that he was here now!

Tagus thundered forward, whirling his rusty sword and deflecting a swing of Torgor's axe. The clang echoed loudly, cannoning off the rows of wooden houses.

"Stay behind me," I gasped, seeing the bigger, stronger minotaur get the upper-hand on Tagus. He batted aside another hack of the Horse-Man's sword, then swung his free arm in a mighty punch that drove Tagus all the way across the dirt road. The Good Beast snarled in pain as his horse ribs slammed into a tree-trunk.

Torgor half-snarled, half-laughed as he loomed over Tagus, axe raised ready for the killing blow.

No!" Before I could intervene to help the Horse-Man, Malvel stepped forward, waving his hands and letting the magic fly wildly in all directions. He had no control over his powers — he simply wanted to protect the Good Beast.

Torgor fled the abandoned town, disappearing into the wilds of Avantia. It would take time, but I would eventually track him down with the help of Epos, and we would banish him back to Gorgonia — where, many years later, Tom and Elenna would do battle with him.

But on this day, I was more concerned with the wayward young Wizard. As King Theo fought his way clear of the collapsed house — and Tagus strode over to us, muscular chest heaving with exertion — young Malvel looked up at me. His expression wore as much confusion as it did excitement at what he had just done.

I gazed back at him, knowing that I had a choice to make. It was within my power to cast a spell on Malvel, to drain him of the magic he possessed. It might have been the safest option for Avantia, to ensure that this unruly youngster did not have the ability to cause chaos in the kingdom. But in using his magic to ward off Torgor, Malvel had shown he had honourable intentions, so I stayed my hand, and told him that His Majesty and I would take him back to the palace, where he would be trained in the arts of Wizardry. In the years to come, the honour Malvel showed that day would desert him, as his thirst for knowledge and power led him to make some terrible choices from which there would be no return. I didn't know it at the time, but I had just taken on a protégé who would grow to become Avantia's greatest ever enemy.

Beast Battle!

One final time, we must return to Mortaxe's Arena. Maximus has brought the Cave Troll Rashouk as his champion, and you must help me select the right Beast to defeat Malvel's son once again.

STRENGTH

Rashouk is five times the width of an average man, making him almost impossible to overpower.

WEAKNESS

Because he lives in the caves of the Dead Peaks, Rashouk never goes outside, and fears bright light - sunshine, lightning, fire are all terrifying to him!

RASHOUK

STRENGTH

Anyone facing Rashouk must avoid his deadly claws — one scratch will turn you into a statue!

AGE:	321
POWER:	165
MAGIC LEVEL:	154
FRIGHT FACTOR:	81

ROKK

AGE:	324
POWER:	250
MAGIC LEVEL:	150
FRIGHT FACTOR:	87

STRENGTH

This Beast is made of rock, which might break Rashouk's claws if the Cave Troll tries to scratch him. He is also even larger than the Evil Beast, which might give him an edge.

WEAKNESS

Rashouk might not be able to scratch Rokk, but he is strong enough to break his limbs. If this happens, the Walking Mountain's whole body could collapse into rubble!

STRENGTH

If Rashouk fears light, there might be no better Beast to fight him than Ellik, whose body can store lightning energy in her blue scales. When fully charged, she can unleash its shocking power!

WEAKNESS

But if she misses with her lightning strike, she will need time to re-charge — and that might give Rashouk enough time to launch a killing strike!

ELLIK

AGE:	287
POWER:	247
MAGIC LEVEL:	177
FRIGHT FACTOR:	85

STRENGTH

This giant bear has claws of his own, as well as fur that might be too thick even for Rashouk's claws...

URSUS

AGE:	172
POWER:	271
MAGIC LEVEL:	179
FRIGHT FACTOR:	90

WEAKNESS

But Ursus is actually a normal bear turned into a Beast by magic. He may not have the experience and fighting instincts to survive a battle against Rashouk...

I know very well how tough Rashouk is, but I would fancy each of these three Beasts chances against him. I'm tempted to employ Rokk, who would pound him into submission, but I can't help thinking that maybe Ellik will terrify the Cave Troll... What should I do?

I think Tom should choose_____

DRAW YOUR OWN SEA-BEAST

Tom's Beast Quests take him to all sorts of dangerous places — frozen plains, searing volcanos, and open plains with nowhere to hide from massive, marauding monsters. But perhaps no Beast Quest is tougher than the one that takes place at sea. One wrong step, and he and Elenna could find themselves submerged in the deep waters — with no way of defending themselves against their attackers. Help Tom and Elenna think of the worst possible dangers to face at sea — even worse than the ones they've already conquered — so that they will be ready for their later oceanic challenges...

The open sea is dangerous enough, but what elements would make a sea-Beast even more deadly?

Don't forget, some water Beasts have additional abilities, making them even trickier opponents — like Balisk the Water Snake, who could divide his own body into two, to launch multiple attacks all at once. What about making yours a Ghost Beast who can become transparent the instant a hero launches a strike with their blade?

- Multiple heads
- Multiple rows of teeth
- Tentacles
- Giant crab pincers
- Sharp fins, possibly made of bone
- Spikes
- Long, forked tails
- Vast length and width
- Power to enslave and control other, smaller sea creatures

I would be lying if I said I have no fear going into a Quest — I often do feel fear, and my Quests at sea are always the most frightening of Quests. If you can imagine a Beast more frightening than ones I've already encountered, that will help me feel a little less afraid should I ever encounter this Beast for real!

SPECIAL QUESTS!

MOST OF THE TIME, WHEN AVANTIA - OR ANOTHER KINGDOM - NEEDS
ME, I KNOW I'M IN FOR NOT JUST ONE QUEST, BUT A SERIES OF THEM,
REPELLING EVIL REPEATEDLY UNTIL IT LEARNS ITS LESSON AND RETREATS.
BUT SOMETIMES, THE DARK WIZARDS WHO ARE MY ENEMIES MAKE MORE
AUDACIOUS ATTEMPTS ON THE KINGDOMS, SUMMONING SOME OF
THE MOST TERRIFYING BEASTS I'VE EVER SEEN. BATTLING EACH OF THESE
MONSTERS JUST ONCE TOOK ALMOST AS MUCH ENERGY AS A SERIES OF QUESTS...

STRENGTH

Mortaxe wields his iron
scythe with deadly skill.
Even if a Quester can
duck under a strike and
get close to Mortaxe, most
of the Skeleton Warrior's
body is covered in a heavy
armour that is impervious
to most blades.

MORTAXE

AGE: 358
POWER: 280
MAGIC LEVEL: 180
FEAR FACTOR: 90

WEAKNESS

His once kind heart
was replaced by that of
a rabid bull-Beast, as
the rage that courses
through him can
make him impulsive.
Impulsive Beasts
occasionally make a
mistake – you might be
able to capitalise!

WEAKNESS

To defeat Viktor, you must
first target Ossator. If you
can damage, or wound, the
skeleton horse, you have a
chance at a fair fight with the
Deadly Archer.

VIKTOR

AGE: 421
POWER: 293
MAGIC LEVEL: 154
FEAR FACTOR: 96

STRENGTH

Viktor is ten feet tall, which gives
him long reach with his cruel blade.
Ossator, his grotesque Skeleton steed,
will charge down any opponent.
Most deadly of all, though, is his
golden bow – get struck by one of his
arrows, and Viktor will claim your
life-force for himself!

OKAWA

AGE:	52
POWER:	295
MAGIC LEVEL:	193
FEAR FACTOR:	97

STRENGTH

One scratch from Okawa's claw will leave you Infected with a deadly sickness, which you can pass onto others. Whole villages can be turned into shambling, mindless minions of Okawa very quickly!

WEAKNESS

The River Beast derives his power from the water he keeps in a hollowed-out crater in his skull. Drain this from his head weakens this terrible Beast!

STRENGTH

Just looking at Ravira can shake the courage of even the most hardened of Questers — the slavering Hounds of Avantia attack on her behalf, always ready to bite a victim and turn them into one of them!

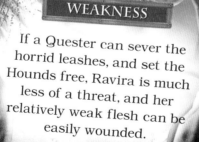

WEAKNESS

If a Quester can sever the horrid leashes, and set the Hounds free, Ravira is much less of a threat, and her relatively weak flesh can be easily wounded.

RAVIRA

AGE:	359
POWER:	291
MAGIC LEVEL:	190
FEAR FACTOR:	91

HISTORY OF MORTAXE

Mortaxe is one of the most complex of Beasts that we have faced. When we did battle with him in his deadly Arena, he was in the grip of a rage that had turned him to Evil, but history records him as a former protector of the kingdom, and ally of Tanner, our first Master. Quite when Evil sunk its teeth into Mortaxe is unknown, but I do hope that, should he ever return, he will be on the side of Good once more…

The Warrior's Road

MARBLE CASTLE

PYRUS

COSHTIN PROVINCE

THE LAST CITY

ERRINEL

ICY MOUNTAIN REGION

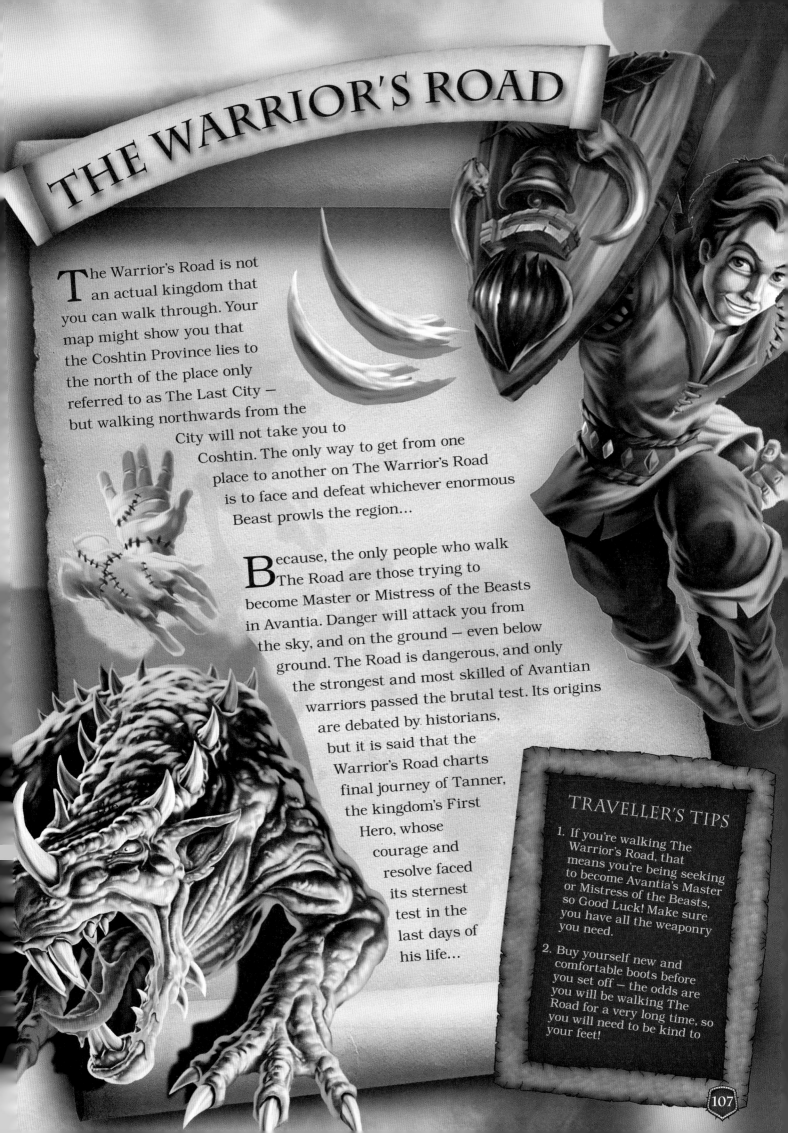

THE WARRIOR'S ROAD

The Warrior's Road is not an actual kingdom that you can walk through. Your map might show you that the Coshtin Province lies to the north of the place only referred to as The Last City — but walking northwards from the City will not take you to Coshtin. The only way to get from one place to another on The Warrior's Road is to face and defeat whichever enormous Beast prowls the region…

Because, the only people who walk The Road are those trying to become Master or Mistress of the Beasts in Avantia. Danger will attack you from the sky, and on the ground — even below ground. The Road is dangerous, and only the strongest and most skilled of Avantian warriors passed the brutal test. Its origins are debated by historians, but it is said that the Warrior's Road charts final journey of Tanner, the kingdom's First Hero, whose courage and resolve faced its sternest test in the last days of his life…

TRAVELLER'S TIPS

1. If you're walking The Warrior's Road, that means you're being seeking to become Avantia's Master or Mistress of the Beasts, so Good Luck! Make sure you have all the weaponry you need.

2. Buy yourself new and comfortable boots before you set off — the odds are you will be walking The Road for a very long time, so you will need to be kind to your feet!

MAP OF YOUR KINGDOM!

One of the things Tom and Elenna can never do without on a Beast Quest is a map — these are crucial not only for making sure that our heroes know they're travelling in the right direction, but also preparing them for the conditions that they may face. With their trusty maps, they never venture into arctic regions without proper clothing, or into deserts without full waterskins. Why don't you draw a map of your own kingdom, just in case Tom and Elenna should ever find themselves there on a Beast Quest?

1. ASK AN ADULT to heat up a cup of water in a microwave, or in a saucepan. Add a tea bag and allow it to stew for at least 10 minutes.

2. While the tea bag is changing the water's colour, fill that time by taking your paper and tearing it around the edges to make it look worn and crumpled — like it's been stuffed in the knapsack of a hero on a dangerous Beast Quest!

3. Allow the tea bag to cool enough so it is safe (and comfortable) for you to handle without burning yourself. Take it out of the water, and squeeze it so that you wring out some of the tea — this way, you won't make the paper too wet and soggy so that it falls apart when you draw on it. Use the tea bag like a paint brush, sweeping it over the paper and turning it a shade of dull brown. It should start to look very old, very quickly!

4. If you want your map to look really old, put the tea bag back in the measuring cup while you allow the first coat to dry. Once it has, take the tea-bag out and repeat Step 3 for a darker colour.

5. Once the paper is completely dry, you're ready to begin drawing your map.

5

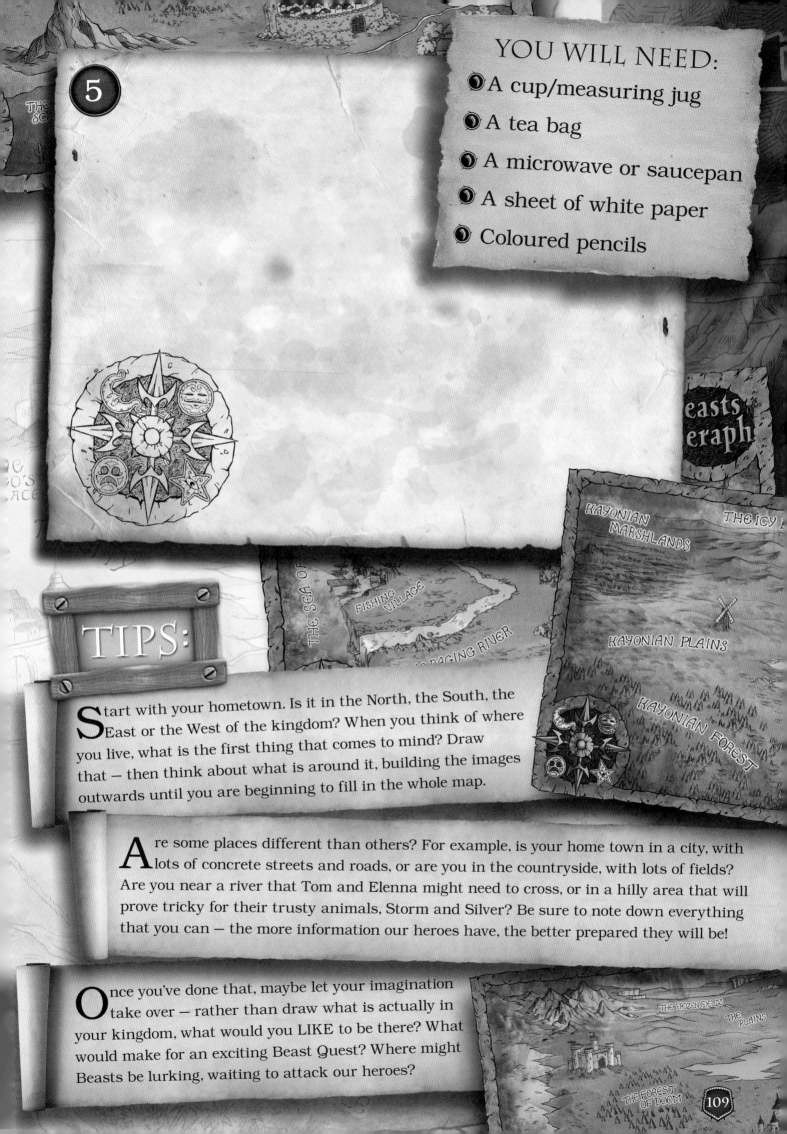

TIPS:

Start with your hometown. Is it in the North, the South, the East or the West of the kingdom? When you think of where you live, what is the first thing that comes to mind? Draw that — then think about what is around it, building the images outwards until you are beginning to fill in the whole map.

Are some places different than others? For example, is your home town in a city, with lots of concrete streets and roads, or are you in the countryside, with lots of fields? Are you near a river that Tom and Elenna might need to cross, or in a hilly area that will prove tricky for their trusty animals, Storm and Silver? Be sure to note down everything that you can — the more information our heroes have, the better prepared they will be!

Once you've done that, maybe let your imagination take over — rather than draw what is actually in your kingdom, what would you LIKE to be there? What would make for an exciting Beast Quest? Where might Beasts be lurking, waiting to attack our heroes?

THE RAID

Being named Master of the Beasts is the greatest honour that can be bestowed on an Avantian warrior — and as the Master, you are expected to face any Quest the kingdom charges you with completing. But there's one Quest that every Master dreads, one place he hopes he will never have to venture to... Grashkor's Chamber of Pain.

Taladon took a deep breath as he steadied his small rowing boat, making sure it did not take on water splashed up by the high waves of Avantia's Western Ocean. In the distance, the fabled Chamber of Pain had just drifted into view, and the sight of its four square turrets rising above jagged battlements plunged a dagger of fear into his heart. Behind these impossibly high walls of grey rock were said to be the deepest, darkest and most unforgiving prison cells anyone could ever imagine.

I don't think I've ever been this nervous on a Quest, he thought. But he steeled himself and plunged his oar back into the water, working it over and over, dragging himself forward to the ominous prison island where the Beast Grashkor was said to guard and torment the worst of Avantia's criminals.

He had been charged with this Quest by King Hugo and Wizard Aduro, and he was not going to let them down. As his boat made contact with the stony island, he guided it through a jagged arch about halfway along the wall, finding himself in a black channel, in which the icy sea air seemed to have got trapped. When he reached a sloping stone jetty, he brought the boat to a stop, unfastening the rope attached to its bow, and tying it as loosely as he could to one of the iron hoops embedded in the stone. He wanted to make sure the boat didn't float away before he could make his escape — but he also knew he might have to make that escape very quickly, so it would not do to leave himself having to untie a complicated knot.

If he made the slightest mistake, Taladon knew he would be trapped here — a prisoner of Grashkor. And legend had it, no one ever escaped this island.

Summoning his courage, Taladon hopped up out of the boat and onto the jetty, drawing his sword as he slowly walked deeper and deeper into Grashkor's prison.

"Arrgghh!" he gasped, almost falling to his knees. A searing, stabbing pain had travelled right through his skull...

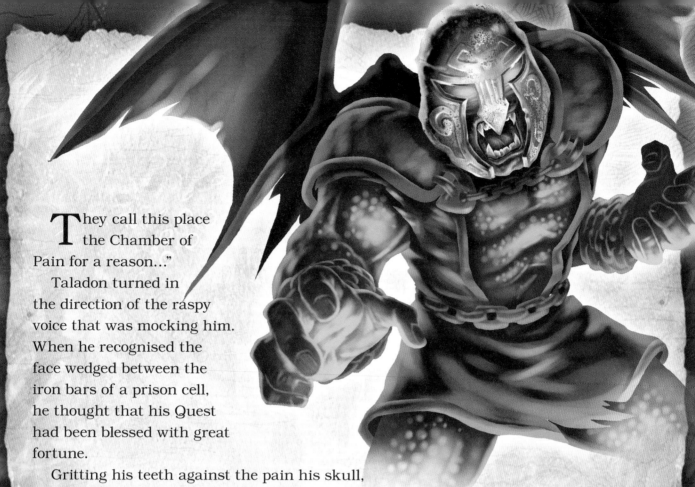

They call this place the Chamber of Pain for a reason…"

Taladon turned in the direction of the raspy voice that was mocking him. When he recognised the face wedged between the iron bars of a prison cell, he thought that his Quest had been blessed with great fortune.

Gritting his teeth against the pain his skull, Taladon said, "I've been sent to here to speak with you, Ned."

"Is that right?" said the prisoner, flashing a smile full of blackened teeth. "And who might you be?"

"Taladon."

Ned gave a laugh, the sound quickly collapsing into a wheeze, and then a cough. The Chamber of Pain was clearly not treating him well. "The famous Master of the Beasts, come to visit wretched old 'Nasty Ned.' I bet I know why he's here to chat with a disgraced former advisor to the king…"

In that moment, Taladon knew the prisoner was not going to be cooperative. But he couldn't worry about that — he was here to retrieve a stolen treasure of Avantia.

"The king wants his father's jewelled necklace back," Taladon told him. "He knows you stole it, when you were banished from the palace. It is precious to His Majesty."

Ned's filthy hands gripped the bars as he pushed his face through them. "And what do I get in return?"

Taladon said nothing. He wasn't here to negotiate with the traitor — and even King Hugo did not have the authority to release prisoners from Grashkor's captivity. The Beast Guard recognised no king or queen.

Ned gave a grim smile, completely lacking humour and goodwill. "I didn't think so," he said. "Good luck making your escape."

As the prisoner turned, Taladon took his chance — he plunged his left arm through the bars and took hold of Ned's shoulder, dragging him back until he was slammed against the cell door. He dropped his sword from his right hand, which he then used to fumble beneath the man's collar, his fingers closing around a metal chain. He snapped it off and drew his arms back.

He had retrieved the green jewelled necklace…

"Grashkor!" Ned bellowed, punching and kicking at the cell door, making as much noise as he can. "Grashkor! There's an intruder in the prison!"

Taladon snatched up his sword and ran back along the prison corridor, only to find his way blocked by Grashkor. The Beast Guard's muscular body was so wide, the walls could barely contain him — which was the only thing that stopped him from lashing his putrid Bull's Skull whip with any power, which gave Taladon enough time to turn around and run in the other direction, dodging the grasping hands of Ned, and then other prisoners, who seemed determined to stop him — perhaps in the hope that they would win favour with their cruel guardian.

As he ran, the pain in Taladon's head got worse, making him stumble on weakened legs. He swiped and swatted at more grasping arms, only to feel an explosion of pain between his shoulder blades as Grashkor's hideous whip struck him and sent him flying forwards. Taladon hit the ground hard, making sure to clutch the jewelled necklace close to his body. There was no way that he could lose this — not after everything he had been through to get it!

When a shadow fell over him, Taladon turned onto his back and looked up at the looming figure of Grashkor.

If he didn't do something soon, his Quest would be over...

As Grashkor loomed, Taladon grit his teeth and gave a growl of determination, backwards-rolling away from a lash of the bone whip. He got to his feet and swiped his sword, trying to sever the bone links — if he could take Grashkor's weapon away, he might stand a chance of defeating the Beast Guard. But Grashkor was too skilled, and wielded his weapon too fast, even in the confined spaces of the prison corridor.

I have to do something, Taladon told himself.

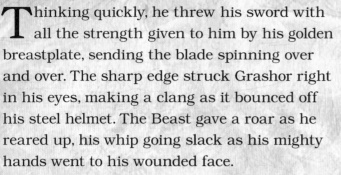

Thinking quickly, he threw his sword with all the strength given to him by his golden breastplate, sending the blade spinning over and over. The sharp edge struck Grashor right in his eyes, making a clang as it bounced off his steel helmet. The Beast gave a roar as he reared up, his whip going slack as his mighty hands went to his wounded face.

Then he lashed them out in a ferocious double-punch that sent Taladon flying back, crashing through one of the prison walls…

…and into the freezing Western Ocean.

Tumbling and spinning beneath the water, Taladon kicked and fought against the tide, but he did not know which way was up. Within seconds, his chest began to burn…

I'm drowning, he thought.

He told himself to fight — that a Master of the Beasts did not give up. But what was there to do? His head still throbbed with the pain of being inside Grashkor's prison, and his limbs had been weakened by the journey and the fight with the Beast Guard.

When he felt a warm, scaly body beneath his, he would have cheered had he been able to. Sepron the Sea Serpent, guardian of the Western Ocean, had come to save him!

Thank you! Taladon clung on tight as Sepron swam fast. He knew the Beast would hear his Master's thoughts.

When they were a safe distance away from Grashkor's prison, Sepron rose up and broke the surface of the water. Taladon took the deepest, most satisfying gulp of air he had ever taken.

Gratefully, he patted Sepron's neck with one hand, still holding the king's jewelled necklace in the other. His Quest had been a success.

"But that's the last time I ever visit Grashkor's prison!"

VILLAINS!

On our Quests, Elenna and I have encountered some terrifying Beasts, but sometimes the purest evil comes in the form of the people controlling the creatures. Two such people were the nefarious duo, Kensa and Sanpao — a Sorceress and a pirate captain, who have tried numerous times to conquer the kingdom.

Little is known about the origins of Kensa and Sanpao's alliance, and if they were to ever tell you the story of how they met, you would be well-advised to not believe them — telling lies and deceiving heroes is one of their favourite things to do!

Tom and Elenna's first encounters with these villains were separate ones, beginning with Sanpao, who was leading his pirate crew on a search for the Tree of Being — the same magical tree that Tom and Elenna needed to find in order to help Freya and Silver make it back to Avantia.

Avantia's heroes succeeded again, and the pirates were locked up in the dungeons for their crimes. Tom and Elenna quickly moved on from worrying about these enemies, for Avantia is constantly threatened by new foes. After chasing the Sorceress Kensa from Henkrall to Avantia, they were stunned when she broke Sanpao free from the dungeon — the two enemies knew each other well. Later, they would discover that they had a daughter (named Ria, who you can read about on page 119), but now Tom and Elenna are always on alert — enemies have a way of surprising you!

KENSA

AGE:	41
POWER:	274
MAGIC LEVEL:	190
FRIGHT FACTOR:	79

SANPAO

AGE:	43
POWER:	265
MAGIC LEVEL:	159
FRIGHT FACTOR:	80

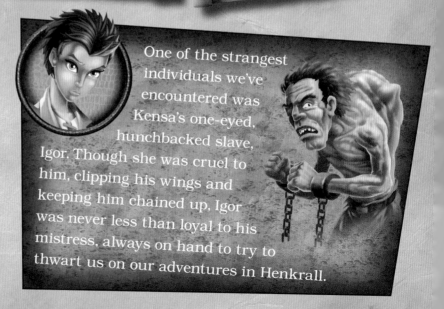

One of the strangest individuals we've encountered was Kensa's one-eyed, hunchbacked slave, Igor. Though she was cruel to him, clipping his wings and keeping him chained up, Igor was never less than loyal to his mistress, always on hand to try to thwart us on our adventures in Henkrall.

Tom's precious yellow jewel gives him an incredibly accurate memory, allowing him to recall all the important details on a Beast Quest. How good is YOUR memory? Study the scene below for ten seconds only, then turn the page and see how many questions you can answer correctly. Good luck!

1. What colour are Tom's eyes?

2. What organ can be seen through the hole in Mortaxe's chest?

3. Is Elenna firing left-handed or right-handed?

4. What weapon does Koraka carry?

5. Which part of Murk's body is constantly on fire?

6. How many potion bottles are there?

7. What is in front of the rock on the bottom right of the page?

Tom and Elenna study up on kingdoms and Beasts whenever they can, but despite this, a Beast Quest can still throw up surprises — like the Beast known as Marlik. Since few have laid eyes on him, no one can agree on his appearance. Here's your chance to influence Avantian opinion — colour in this image of Marlik the Drowning Terror. How scary can you make him look?

HEROES OF HISTORY

A kingdom under constant threat from Dark Magic, and Beasts lurking beyond its borders needs all the heroes it can get, and Avantia has been graced by some true braves over the course of its history. I am proud to follow in their footsteps, and strive every day to live up to their legends...

History records a boy named Tanner rising as Avantia's fabled "First Hero" — who travelled the kingdom, gathering companions to lead a resistance against the vicious warlord named Derthsin, who was on a mission to find the mythical Mask of Death. Said to be made from the flesh of Anoret — a Beast so ancient, nobody is sure how old she is — the Mask was said to be filled with impossible power. Any who wore it would have the power to control the kingdom's Beasts...

After the era of the First Hero passed, so too did the era of Beasts. Rarely seen, over time they became myth and legend — subjects of exciting stories parents told their children... stories that nobody really believed. Eventually, only a select group of Avantians were allowed to know the truth — kings, queens, Wizards... and the Master or Mistress of the Beasts.

The people of Avantia would soon be saddled with a preoccupation that took precedence over their fascination with "old legends" — war. Time and again, over the decades and centuries, the kingdom would be bruised, wounded and scarred by conflict as armies waged wars on each other. It is a testament to the honour inherent in all Avantians that their greatest warriors never summoned the Beasts that were loyal to them, despite the fact that one gust of fiery dragon breath, or swipe of a mountain giant's enormous fist, could have won them any battle.

Most Masters and Mistresses of the Beasts are recorded by history for their exploits on the battlefield, so that the people know of their heroics, despite not knowing the full story. There are legendary figures like Cristof the Fierce, who wielded an iron flail on the battlefields when a savage rebel army from the east crossed the unforgiving Forbidden Land in an effort to invade Avantia. And there are also heroines like Bethan the Mighty — a warrior woman who, legend has it, stood seven feet tall and bore a broadsword too heavy for even the strongest man to lift.

But there are some whose stories simply... stop. Like Kara, a Mistress who fought sixty years before Tom set off on his first Quest. Not even the kingdom's Wizards know why she set off towards the Western Ocean one day, to never return. Many theories have been put forth to explain her mysterious disappearance, the most grisly being that she was somehow "fused" with the Beast that she was battling...

THE FUTURE...

In the future, Elenna and I run a Knight's Academy, training Avantia's newest young warriors, to make sure that the kingdom has a number of new protectors, who can stand up to Evil. This is very important, because Elenna and I are not always around to fight for the kingdom — and we won't be around forever. Avantia will need all the heroes it can get, and these three youngsters proved themselves worthy defenders when Malvel's dastardly son, Maximus, turned up in Avantia to cause trouble. One-by-one, they undertook Quests of their own, to tame a Good Beast and ride it into battle against our newest enemy...

SAM

It was tough for Sam to leave his home village, Littleton, and travel to The City, but he was not going to turn down an invitation from Tom, Master of the Beasts. So he rode his horse, Warrior, all the way across the kingdom, and led Epos in a battle against a bewitched Ferno...

AGE: 12
POWER: 187
MAGIC LEVEL: 103
FEAR FACTOR: 40

EVAN

Hailing from the Dark Jungle, Evan proved her bravery by posing as her twin brother, Owen — who could not accept Tom's invitation because of his broken leg. Evan soon proved that she belonged among the young Knights, using her folding spear to great effect as she worked to free Amictus from Maximus's enchantment.

AGE: 12
POWER: 189
MAGIC LEVEL: 107
FEAR FACTOR: 38

WILL

This young hero, from Shipton-on-Sea, proved that he had the focus of a seasoned warrior when he was chosen to be the third Knight to battle Maximus. Having trained hard, Will was more than ready to lead Sepron in an oceanic battle against the six-headed Narga, and showed a hero's accuracy with the Golden Trident!

AGE: 13
POWER: 192
MAGIC LEVEL: 102
FEAR FACTOR: 41

THE FUTURE CONTINUED

As time goes on, Avantia will gain more than heroes – it will gain new enemies, too. The battle between Good and Evil is not done yet, and these are the villains on whom we must keep a close eye...

MAXIMUS

AGE:	13
POWER:	192
MAGIC LEVEL:	102
FEAR FACTOR:	41

The spiteful, vengeful son of the Dark Wizard Malvel, Maximus is the latest threat to Avantia's security, and launched a crafty attack on the kingdom by stealing one of the golden gauntlets from the palace armoury, which he used to bend Beasts, both Good and Evil, to his will. After taming first Ferno, then Amictus, he took his villainy to the seas and found a faithful sidekick in Ria, the daughter of the Sorceress Kensa and the Pirate King, Sanpao.

A former Apprentice of Malvel's, Petra now walks the line between Enemy and Ally. The daughter of the wicked Witch, Kapra, Petra's upbringing was a dark one, but lately there have been signs that she is discovering the Good within herself. If she commits to that side of her character, she will be able to achieve great things as a Good Witch.

PETRA

AGE:	16
POWER:	120
MAGIC LEVEL:	120
FEAR FACTOR:	40

RIA

This cloaked girl followed in her parents' footsteps, in that she was both villainous and fond of using nasty Dark Magic. No ingredient was too disgusting for her, not even Beast-eggs (even if she and Maximus disagreed over whether they belonged to the First Beast!). The strange, oily black potion that she wore in a vial around her neck created a whirlpool in the sea that almost sucked down Beasts and ships!

YOUR ROLE ON A BEAST QUEST

WHAT IF YOU WERE CALLED UP TO DEFEND YOUR KINGDOM IN A TIME OF CRISIS? TAKE THIS QUIZ TO DETERMINE HOW YOU WOULD BEST SERVE YOUR REALM...

QUESTION 1: WHAT WOULD YOU DO IF YOU WERE ON A SHIP, LOST AT SEA?

Ⓐ First things first — make sure that everyone is calm, and that there are no leaks on board.

Ⓑ Cast a net to catch some fish — just in case you're stuck out here for a long time!

Ⓒ Make a decision on a course and set sail — you refuse to let your Quest sink without a trace.

QUESTION 2: ON A QUEST THAT'S TAKEN YOU TO A JUNGLE, YOU WALK INTO A SWARM OF INSECTS. HOW DO YOU SAVE YOURSELF?

Ⓐ Run as fast as you can in another direction to lure them away from your friends.

Ⓑ Light a fire — the smoke will drive them away.

Ⓒ Throw up your shield and keep moving forward. You don't take backwards steps!

QUESTION 3: YOU HAVE BEEN MAKING YOUR WAY THROUGH A NETWORK OF CAVES, BUT YOU HAVE DROPPED YOUR TORCH AND NOW HAVE NO LIGHT. WHAT DO YOU DO?

Ⓐ Retrace your steps, back to the cave entrance so that you can regroup and figure out how you're going to get around this problem.

Ⓑ Put your hand on your friend's shoulder as you continue to make your way through the cave. It's safer that way.

Ⓒ Hold your sword higher, and stretched out further. Walk with slower, quieter footsteps so that you can better hear if anything is lurking in the shadows.

QUESTION 4: YOU ARE FACE-TO-FACE WITH A GIANT BEAST WHOSE JAWS CAN SWALLOW YOU AND YOUR FRIENDS WHOLE. HOW DO YOU TACKLE THIS CHALLENGE?

Ⓐ   Retreat — if you can see ALL of the Beast, you can better anticipate where its attack is coming from.

Ⓑ   Let it get a little closer — so you don't have to aim so far with your bow and arrow!

Ⓒ   Ask your friends to distract it so that you can sneak around and take the Beast's back.

QUESTION 5: ALONG THE ROAD, YOU REALISE THAT THE SOLE OF YOUR BOOT HAS STARTED TO WEAR AWAY. WHAT DO YOU DO?

Ⓐ   Keep an eye out for a nearby town — you might be able to buy (or barter for) a replacement.

Ⓑ   Tear a strip from your sleeve and place that in your boot to cover any holes. You can get new boots after you get home.

Ⓒ   Pick up the pace — the sooner you complete this Quest, the sooner you can deal with the discomfort.

QUESTION 6: IT'S RAINING TOO HEAVY FOR YOU TO MAKE A FIRE — YOU CAN'T COOK THE FOOD YOU'VE CAUGHT. HOW DO YOU DEAL WITH YOUR HUNGER?

Ⓐ   Suggest that you scout for any fruit that might be nearby. It might be wet, but at least it doesn't need to be cooked!

Ⓑ   Find some shelter so that you can eat the bread you made sure to stash in your knapsack before you set off.

Ⓒ   Cover up and wait it out. It can't rain forever, and a good, hearty meal will give you more strength for the journey ahead — which might be the difference between success and failure.

QUESTION 7: SANPAO AND HIS DASTARDLY PIRATES HAVE SET FIRE TO THE ARMOURY IN KING HUGO'S PALACE – YOUR WEAPONS ARE IN THERE! WHAT DO YOU DO NOW?

Ⓐ   Shut the door and raise the alarm — the fire needs to be contained!

Ⓑ   Assess the situation before making a decision. If you can retrieve your weapons, you will — but not with unnecessary risk!

Ⓒ   Tie a wet cloth around your face so that you can safely breathe — you're going in there to get your weapons!

IF YOU ANSWERED...

MOSTLY A'S

You are a supportive friend — like Wilfred. You're a valued advisor.

MOSTLY B'S

You are sharp-witted, like Elenna. Anyone would want you by their side.

MOSTLY C'S

You are courageous, and without fear — like Tom. You are most likely to be leading the Quest!

One of the most terrifying Beasts that Tom ever faced was Raksha the Mirror Demon, who was able to absorb the strengths of Avantia's Good Beasts into himself. Here's your chance to bring this exciting – but frightening – scene to life! Use pencils or crayons to colour in the scene pictured here.

We hope you've enjoyed tackling our fiendish activities — and learning about not just our past Quests, but stories from Avantia's long history. We have a feeling the future will be just as storied — there are surely still many more Quests ahead.

While there's blood in our veins, Elenna and I will continue to fight for the kingdom — we hope we can always count on your support...

Until next time, farewell — and stay brave!

Tom

ANSWERS

Page 30

The kingdom of: SERAPH

Page 31

Page 48

GUESS THE IMPOSTOR

Reader, I need your help! Tom and I are battling Koba, Ghost of the Shadows, but the 400-year-old Beast has transformed himself into Tom, and I need to figure out which one is my real best friend! Study the two pictures closely – one of them is the real Tom, and one is Koba in disguise. You need to help me find all five clues that will reveal the Beastly impostor!

PLEASE LOOK VERY CAREFULLY! WE DON'T WANT ELENNA TO ATTACK THE WRONG ME!

1. Missing Bell Token
2. Green Eyes
3. Missing belt gems
4. Ear Rings
5. Red Hair

Page 88

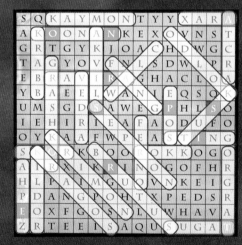

Beasts: SPIROS and ANORET

Page 89

ESCAPE THE MAZE!

Disaster! The Ghost-Beasts have escaped the Forbidden Land, and have cornered Elenna in a terrifying maze. It's so dark in there that she can't see very well – a Beast could be around any corner.

You must guide her safely out of the maze to where Tom is waiting for her – but be careful to avoid the Ghost Beasts. One wrong turn, and Elenna will be walking right into her doom!

Page 46

1. A: Ferno
2. C: Zepha, in the Western Ocean
3. B: That she will turn you to stone
4. A: Making their two heads fight each other
5. C: Koba
6. B: Terra
7. C: A bounty hunter looking to capture the Horse-Man
8. A. Six
9. B. Ellik
10. A: Cornix

Page 116

1. Blue
2. Heart
3. Right
4. Spear
5. Head
6. Two
7. Map

Congratulations on making it to the end of your Quest. You've shown great courage to read about fearsome, terrifying Beasts – and your adventurous spirit is certainly not in doubt. Now, see how well your knowledge of the Quests served you on some of the fiendish quizzes in this Annual. Check your answers here!